"I don't want you to go."

Sara inched closer to Cruz and her scent hypnotized him.

"If I stay..." He couldn't make himself say the words.

"I know." Her eyes softened. "Let's take it one day at a time."

He'd been forced to take it one day at a time in prison, and that was the last thing he wanted to do with Sara. But he was just a man. A man who yearned to be with a woman who would make him feel good inside. And worthy.

"I'm not asking for anything more from you. I just..." She dropped her gaze for a moment, then looked him in the eye. "I just need you here." Her voice cracked, and he nearly lost the battle to stand firm.

"I can't stay." He stepped by her and headed for the barn. He didn't know whether he was a fool or a coward. The one thing he knew for sure was that he was no saint.

Dear Reader,

In December 2011 *A Rodeo Man's Promise* was released as part of my Rodeo Rebels series (the book is available in ebook). I'm thrilled to share that the three delinquent teens in *A Rodeo Man's Promise* will get their own stories in my new series, Cowboys of the Rio Grande.

A Cowboy's Redemption is Cruz Rivera's story. Cruz showed great potential for rodeo and was set to ride the circuit when one fateful night he made a decision that changed his world and landed him in prison, robbing him of a rodeo career.

We've all made mistakes, and many of us would do things differently if we could go back in time. But there are no do-overs in life—we can only move forward. Having served his prison sentence, Cruz is searching for peace and a new purpose for his life when he runs into widow Sara Mendez and her daughter, Dani. They tempt Cruz to believe he deserves happiness, but deep down he doesn't feel worthy of their love and trust—not when he's carrying a secret that he's certain will change the way Sara feels about him.

I hope you enjoy Cruz and Sara's journey as they show us that the healing power of love redeems us all.

You can find more information on the books I write at my website, marinthomas.com, as well as links to all my social media hangouts.

I love hearing from readers and can be reached at marin@marinthomas.com.

Happy reading,

Marin

A COWBOY'S REDEMPTION

—

Marin Thomas

HARLEQUIN® AMERICAN ROMANCE®

Recycling programs
for this product may
not exist in your area.

ISBN-13: 978-0-373-75572-1

A Cowboy's Redemption

Copyright © 2015 by Brenda Smith-Beagley

Printed in U.S.A.

Marin Thomas grew up in the Midwest, then attended college at the U of A in Tucson, Arizona, where she earned a BA in radio-TV and played basketball for the Lady Wildcats. Following graduation she married her college sweetheart in the historic Little Chapel of the West in Las Vegas, Nevada. Recent empty nesters Marin and her husband now live in Texas, where cattle is king, cowboys are plentiful and pickups rule the road.

Books by Marin Thomas

Harlequin American Romance

The Cash Brothers

The Cowboy Next Door
Twins Under the Christmas Tree
Her Secret Cowboy
The Cowboy's Destiny
True Blue Cowboy
A Cowboy of Her Own

Rodeo Rebels

Rodeo Daddy
The Bull Rider's Secret
A Rodeo Man's Promise
Arizona Cowboy
A Cowboy's Duty
No Ordinary Cowboy

Visit the Author Profile page at Harlequin.com for more titles.

To my cousin Jeanna, who is always on the lookout for my newest release—thank you for reading my books. I love you.

Prologue

"This rodeo won't be the same without you, Rivera."

Cruz Rivera's gaze skipped over the prison warden, Mitchell Bole, who stopped at his side near the bronc-busting chutes. The first rule Cruz had learned on the inside was that you never made eye contact with the warden.

"Your talent has turned our little rodeo into a money-making machine."

Before Cruz had arrived at the White Sands New Mexico Correctional Facility, the prison rodeo had been nothing more than a two-hour afternoon show for the best-behaved inmates. After Cruz had proved his talents on the back of a bronc, the prison's athletic director had convinced the warden to grant special privileges to the most agile convicts. As a reward for good behavior the men were allowed to practice their rodeo skills on a weekly basis.

Cruz stood out among the other convicts—most likely he'd inherited his abilities from his father, who'd been a national champion bull rider back in the day. As word had spread through the local community that the prison had a bona fide rodeo cowboy, citizens had begun showing up to watch the practices. The warden saw an opportunity to make a quick buck and opened the event to the public. Over a thousand people had turned out for the first rodeo. Men, women and children sat on the tailgates of their trucks or the hoods of their cars, watching from behind a chain-link fence decorated with razor wire. Each year the crowd grew larger and eventually the warden commissioned a construction company to build a three-thousand-seat arena. That year, sponsors signed up to support the rodeo and pretty soon the inmates who didn't compete were enlisted to make crafts—leather products like wallets and belts and original prison artwork— that were sold at the event.

"Monroe is your new star," Cruz said.

"He's not half as good-looking as you." Bole winked.

Cruz wasn't a vain man, but he'd caught his reflection in the sliver of glass that posed as a window in his cell door. He was no longer a fresh-faced kid. Twelve years at White Sands had hardened him. Time had hollowed out his face, making his cheekbones and jaw more pronounced. And thanks to a fall off a nasty bronc four years ago, his nose was crooked. His chiseled looks combined with his dark hair and eyes had garnered plenty of looks from the female rodeo groupies. Each year his buckle-bunny fan club grew in numbers, the ladies taunting Cruz and the other inmates with their skimpy clothing, big hair and lipstick-painted mouths.

"You never know." The warden chuckled. "You might get caught breaking a rule and we'll have to extend your stay…"

Again.

After the warden had realized Cruz's value to the

prison's bottom line, he hadn't wanted him leaving. When Cruz came up for parole, Bole had made sure he didn't go anywhere. The warden had sent Scorpion to deal with Cruz. The rapist cornered Cruz, forcing him to defend himself from a sexual assault. The incident had added eight years to his sentence.

"Are you sure you want to do that?" Cruz said.

Bole narrowed his eyes.

"The fans know this is my last rodeo. If I don't make parole, a reporter might show up at the prison asking why."

"There are ways to keep reporters from knowing everything that goes on behind these walls."

"And there are ways to get information to the public without you being aware." Cruz grinned. "I worked hard to make you the most envied prison warden in New Mexico. I can work just as hard to take you down."

Bole's face turned ashen even as the lines bracketing his mouth deepened. "You just make sure you win today. Got that?"

"Yes, sir."

After Bole walked off, Cruz closed his eyes and cleared his mind of all the trash that clogged it. Years of garbage had accumulated inside his head, and shoving the bad experiences and memories aside wasn't easy. With extra effort he envisioned his draw—a bronc named High Wire. If he made it to eight, he'd advance to the second go-round later in the afternoon. If he won that one, he'd make it to the championship round in the evening.

He needed three victories today to become the first inmate to win the saddle-bronc event twelve straight years.

Then he'd retire his spurs for good.

"Ladies and gentlemen, welcome to the sixteenth annual White Sands prison rodeo!"

Noise from the crowd echoed through the arena as Cruz put on his spurs and riding glove. In the past he'd never worn one of the Kevlar vests the prison supplied—mostly because he hadn't given a crap if he'd gotten injured or killed. But his parole hearing was next week and he was having second thoughts about wearing the extra protection. Then he nixed the idea— it was bad karma to change his routine.

"This is the event you've all been waiting for—our saddle-bronc competition." Once the crowd quieted, the announcer—a prison guard named Larry—gave spectators a rundown of the event rules.

Cruz stood by himself next to High Wire's chute. There wasn't a whole lot of camaraderie among prison rodeo contenders. It was what it was—a group of sex offenders, murderers, armed robbers and drug lords playing cowboy for the day. As soon as the crowd disappeared and they hauled the roughstock away, the cowboys morphed back into society's outcasts and returned to their cells.

Except for Cruz. He'd get out of this hell hole in three days.

"We know who you want to see ride," the announcer said. "Turn your attention to chute number three, where Cruz Rivera is getting ready to battle High Wire!"

Cruz climbed the slats and waved the cowboy hat he'd been given for the day at the crowd. He nodded to the buckle bunnies holding signs with their phone numbers. Twelve years was a long time to go without sex and he looked forward to one day holding a pretty lady in his arms again.

"I know Rivera is a favorite among the ladies. Let's see if this cowboy can tame High Wire—a bronc famous for his acrobatics."

Cruz slid his leg over the gelding and found his seat. The horse trembled with anticipation. He checked over his shoulder—Bole stood a few feet away, his eyes always moving. Always watching. Cruz adjusted his grip on the six-foot hack rein and willed his racing heart to slow to a steady beat. On the count of three he nodded to the gateman and the chute opened.

High Wire bolted from the enclosure. His back legs extended and Cruz pitched forward but managed to mark out despite the awkward position. Saddle-bronc busting was akin to ballet and Cruz had been born with balance and rhythm. Unlike the other rodeo events, saddle bronc relied less on strength and more on timing and finesse.

Unbeknownst to High Wire, Cruz took control of the ride. With each buck he leaned forward straight up the bronc's neck to the rigging, then right back down. No jerky movements. He squared his shoulders and held his free arm high and steady.

When the buzzer sounded, the roar of the crowd threatened to disrupt Cruz's concentration and he doubled down, putting in extra effort while he waited for the right opening to dismount. The opportunity came and went and Cruz remained on High Wire. A part of him didn't want the ride to end. If he could have stayed on High Wire the rest of his days he might have found his utopia. But that was not how a convict's life worked—he didn't get to make the calls.

High Wire was tiring—the bronc had been through enough for one day and Cruz launched himself off the animal. He hit the ground and rolled, coming to his feet in one fluid motion. He retrieved his hat from the dirt, then waved it at the crowd.

One ride down. Two to go.

Then he could get on with the rest of his life— wherever that took him.

Chapter One

On a Monday afternoon in mid-May, Cruz clutched the plastic bag that held his few belongings and waited for the prison guards to buzz the tower. The massive gates yawned open and he walked away from the hellhole that had been his home for far too long.

Ignoring the clanking sound of the iron bars closing behind him, he breathed deeply, filling his lungs with hot, dusty air. Crazy, but he swore the oxygen in the parking lot smelled a whole lot sweeter than it did inside the prison yard behind him.

Let it go, man. You're thirty-one years old. The best days are yet to come.

From here on out whatever road he traveled would be better than the one he'd been on for over a decade. He shoved his hand inside his pants pocket and clutched the fifty dollars in gate money and the bus ticket to Las Cruces. The Greyhound passed by the prison three times a week. He had fifteen minutes to make the half-mile walk to the highway and catch the bus. But damned if he could get his feet to move. He checked over his shoulder. The guards stood sentry, their faces expressionless. The gray-bar hotel sucked the life out of everyone who worked or lived within its walls.

His cell mate, Orlando, had been in and out of prison most of his adult life and had warned Cruz that he might freeze up on the outside. Cruz had hated prison with every fiber of his being but it had been predictable—even comfortable in a perverse way. He'd been told what to do, how to do it and when to do it for the past 4,326 days. There was no one on this side of the wall instructing him to do anything. From now on every decision was in his hands.

"Need a lift?"

Cruz's heart jumped inside his chest but not a muscle twitched—years of bracing himself for an unexpected attack had taught him to control his body's reactions. It took only a few seconds for the familiar voice to register, then Cruz relaxed. *Riley Fitzgerald.* He grinned at the former world-champion saddle-bronc rider—the only man who'd ever tried to make a difference in Cruz's life.

"Considering where you just came from, you look good." Fitzgerald clasped Cruz's shoulder and gave him a hug. The last hug he'd received had been from Maria Alvarez, Fitzgerald's wife and Cruz's former high-school teacher, after he'd passed the tests required to earn his GED. She'd been proud of him that day— too bad he'd let her down. "How's Maria?" She and Fitzgerald ran the Juan Alvarez Ranch for Boys outside Albuquerque. The ranch had been named after Maria's deceased younger brother, who'd been killed in a gang shooting when he was a teen.

"Maria's fine. She's eager to see you."

Cruz wasn't ready to socialize with people. Not yet. Not until he grew acclimated to life outside of prison.

"There's a job waiting for you at the ranch," Fitzgerald said.

"What kind of job?"

"Counseling troubled teens."

Cruz had spent more than a decade behind bars and the experience had left him jaded. He was the last person who should mentor gangbangers.

"Thanks, but I'll pass." Last week Cruz had met with his parole officer and had been handed a laundry list of do's and don'ts—the most important being that he stay the hell away from Albuquerque and gangs. Fine by him. There was nothing left in the barrio but bad memories. Cruz was free to move about the state as long as he reported in to his parole officer on a weekly basis.

"What are your plans?" Fitzgerald asked.

"I don't have any yet."

"We both know what you're qualified to do."

Rodeo. Cruz had promised himself that when he left prison he'd never ride again. What had once been a dream—becoming a world-champion saddle-bronc rider—had been stolen from him the moment the gun had gone off in his hand.

He'd had a hell of a rodeo run in prison and his prowess in the saddle had earned him the respect of the inmates and guards and those living in the surrounding community. But no matter how accomplished he'd become, he was still a felon cowboy and his victories were tainted.

"I've had my fill of rodeo," Cruz said. All he wanted now was to be by himself and reclaim the sense of peace that had been ripped from him when the judge had handed down his sentence.

"If you won't accept the job then you're going to need these." Fitzgerald dropped a set of keys in Cruz's hand.

"Shorty wanted you to have his wheels." Fitzgerald pointed to an older-model red Ford parked next to a Dodge Ram with a man sitting in the front seat—probably an employee from the ranch.

Before Cruz found his voice, Fitzgerald said, "I'd better get on the road. We have a group of boys arriving in a few days and Maria's got me busy until then." He shook Cruz's hand. "I'll tell her that you'll visit soon."

When Fitzgerald reached his vehicle, Cruz called out, "You hear much from Alonso or Victor these days?"

"Come out to the ranch and Maria will fill you in on the guys." Fitzgerald hopped into the Dodge and drove off, leaving Cruz alone.

Alone was good. Alone was his normal. Even among the thousands of prisoners he'd lived with daily, he'd always been alone.

He stared at the Ford. The sun glinted off the shiny paint, highlighting minor dings and scratches on the doors. Fitzgerald must have run the pickup through a car wash on the way to the prison. As he crossed the lot an image of Shorty popped into his head—gray hair, scruffy beard, bow-legged and cheek swollen with chewing tobacco. The retired bullfighter could spit tobacco juice twenty-five feet through the air.

Cruz pressed the key fob and unlocked the truck. He slid behind the wheel, then remembered he didn't have a valid driver's license. He'd have to remedy that sooner rather than later. He rummaged through the glove compartment and discovered the truck's title—it was in Fitzgerald's name. Cruz assumed Fitzgerald was paying the insurance on the vehicle. He shut the glove box then started the engine. The needle on the gas gauge registered a full tank—enough fuel to get him the hell away from this place by the end of the day.

He turned on the air conditioning and adjusted the vents toward his face. Freedom was feeling more real every second. When he buckled his seat belt, he noticed the envelope sitting on the passenger seat with his name scrawled on the front. He tore open the seal and removed the handwritten note.

If yer reading this, son, then I must be ten feet under in the boot yard. I was hoping I'd be there to greet ya when ya got out of the slammer but the ol ticker must have quit ticking.

Cruz's eyes watered. Damn Shorty for dying. *What the hell, man? Did you think life wouldn't go on for others while you were in prison?* Yes. No. *Shit.*

I ain't never spent time in prison, but I had a friend who did and it took a while fer him to get used to being free. Ya gotta stay out of trouble, son. The best place fer ya is the circuit. Ya keep riding just like ya did in prison and before ya know it, yer pent-up anger n pain'll disappear.

Cruz rubbed his eyes, ignoring the moisture that leaked onto his fingertips.

*I made sure Fitzgerald set ya up proper-like fer
the next go-round. Do me proud, son. That's all
I ask. See ya on the other side—but not too soon,
ya hear?*
Shorty.

Cruz glanced into the backseat. A Stetson sat next to
brand-new rodeo gear, including a saddle for bronc riding. Next to the gear rested a duffel bag. He unzipped
the canvas. Several pairs of jeans, shirts, underwear
and socks were packed inside along with a Ziploc bag
of toiletries. A belt and pair of cowboy boots rested on
the floor. Had Shorty paid for all this?

A sharp stab of guilt pricked Cruz. Each year he'd
rodeoed for the prison, he'd given the warden a list of
people he wanted to deny entrance to—Fitzgerald and
his wife, Maria, and Shorty—because he'd let them
down and he didn't have the guts to face them. And
his two best friends, Alonso and Vic. Alonso because
he couldn't bear to see the sympathy in his eyes, and
Vic because he should have been the one sitting in
prison—not Cruz.

Included in the envelope was a list of summer rodeos. Shorty had backed Cruz into a corner. The last
thing he wanted to do was ride another bronc, but out
of respect for the old man, he'd rodeo until he figured
out what to do with his life.

First things first. He needed a job. The fifty dollars in his pocket wouldn't last long. His best bet was
to look for work in a city like Las Cruces. Instead, he
drove west, hoping to find temporary employment on
a ranch or a farm. As soon as he earned enough money

to keep the gas tank filled and pay a handful of entry fees, he'd hit the circuit.

Cruz drove over two hours before giving in to the gnawing hunger in his gut. When he whizzed past a billboard displaying a faded and tattered advertisement for Sofia's Mexican Cantina in Papago Springs, he took the exit and drove the frontage road for a mile before arriving in the one-horse town.

The two-block map dot consisted of abandoned mobile homes and bankrupt businesses. The gas station's single pump was missing its hose and the attached convenience store was packed from floor to ceiling with junk. Behind the station an antiques shop and Cut & Dry Hair Salon sat vacant.

The only two places that appeared open for business were The Pony Soldier—a bar with a life-size plaster horse spinning on a pole attached to the roof—and Sofia's Mexican Cantina, which was located inside an adobe house. Next to the restaurant sat a corral with two donkeys and a horse, a lean-to, a barn and a rusted, windowless single-wide trailer. A newer SUV was parked alongside a battered pickup in front of the home.

He'd dreamed of his first meal as a free man taking place at a Waffle House. His mouth watered when he thought of how long it had been since he'd eaten homemade biscuits and gravy. But it appeared he was destined—at least for today—to eat what he'd eaten in prison, more bland refried beans and rice. He parked next to the SUV and noticed a Help Wanted sign in the window of the restaurant.

He knocked but no one answered. When he tested the knob, the door opened. The smell of chorizo and fry bread assaulted his nose and he forgot all about biscuits and gravy. The front room had been converted into a waiting area. He tapped the bell on the counter to announce his presence. A beautiful blonde with blue eyes and an engaging smile appeared out of nowhere.

"Hello." Her feminine voice sounded foreign to Cruz and he thought for a moment that he'd imagined it. "Welcome to Sofia's Mexican Cantina." She peered behind him. "Are you dining alone?"

Temporarily speechless, he nodded.

"Right this way."

The subtle sway of her feminine hips mesmerized him as he followed her into another room. She ushered him to the table by the window, which looked out at the donkeys and the lone horse. He cleared his throat. "Thank you."

She held out a laminated menu. "My name is Sara Mendez."

Her smile and twinkling blue eyes shot his concentration to smithereens. It had been a long time since he'd been this close to a pretty woman.

"If you're not in a hurry, José will cook anything you want."

Oh, man, he was so *not* in a hurry.

"His specialty is pork tamales and chicken enchiladas."

Hopefully anything José cooked would be better than the prison slop he'd consumed. "I'll take a tamale and an enchilada."

"You won't be disappointed." She hurried off, her long ponytail swinging behind her.

Left alone he stared out the window, watching the animals in the corral. He'd thought a lot about the day he'd finally be free from prison and none of the scenarios he'd imagined had been anywhere close to this.

And today wasn't over with.

His ears caught the sound of shoes scuffing against the floor and he spotted a miniature shadow ducking out of sight behind the doorway. Sara returned with a basket of chips, homemade salsa and a glass of water.

"I apologize for not taking your drink order." Her cheeks turned pink, and he wondered if he made her nervous—and not in a good way. Could people tell he'd just been released from prison?

"I'll take a beer—" He'd better not drink alcohol in case he got pulled over by the highway patrol. "Make that a Coke."

"Coming right up." As soon as she left, the tiny shadow darted from the doorway and hid behind a chair. He munched on a chip, waiting for the little spy to show herself. He didn't wait long before she popped up next to him. The sprite had dark pigtails and brown eyes.

"My name is Dani. What's yours?"

"Cruz."

"Cruz?" She pulled out the chair next to him and climbed onto the seat. "That's a funny name. I'm five years old. How old are you?"

"Thirty-one."

"That's really old. Do you know my grandpa?"

"No, I don't." The child was pure innocence, reminding Cruz not to get too close.

"My papa's a good cook."

Cruz pushed the basket of chips toward Dani. "Help yourself."

She grabbed a chip and took tiny bites with her tiny teeth. "My daddy died."

Shocked at her blunt statement, Cruz fumbled for something to say. "I'm sorry."

"Mama wants Papa to come live with us."

Pity for the child and her mother filled Cruz, surprising him. He hadn't believed he had any compassion left in him, but the little girl's sweetness tugged at a place deep inside him—a place he'd shut the door on as soon as he'd been locked up inside the prison walls.

"Dani." The blonde returned. "I'm sorry. My daughter is a chatterbox and we don't get many customers." She set the meal and drink on the table then brushed a strand of hair from Dani's face. "You miss your friends back home, don't you?"

Cruz wanted to ask where home was but didn't.

Dani pointed. "Cruz can be my friend."

Sara quirked an eyebrow and he felt as if he'd just been reprimanded. He held out his hand. "Cruz Rivera." She shook his hand and the calluses on her palm surprised him.

"Nice to meet you." Sara switched her attention to her daughter. "Go into the kitchen and help Papa with the dishes." Sara grabbed her daughter's hand and helped her from the chair, then they left him to eat in peace.

Cruz savored his first bite of real food, letting the spices soak into his tongue before chewing. A lump formed in his throat as he swallowed. Once the first bite hit his stomach, he devoured the meal.

"Oh, my," Sara said when she returned with a water pitcher and gaped at his empty plate. "You must have been starving."

"It was real good."

"I'll make sure to tell my father-in-law."

Without asking a single question Cruz knew more about the lives of three strangers than he knew about himself anymore. Sara set the bill down and walked off.

He left a twenty on the table, then stood. He didn't want to wait for his change—a hefty tip would be his first good deed since leaving prison. He snuck out of the house, hopped into Shorty's truck, then started the engine and flipped on the AC. Then he sat and stared at the damned donkeys.

After five minutes he shut off the truck and entered the restaurant where he found Sara clearing his table. Their gazes met across the room. Man, her eyes were pretty.

You're asking for trouble.

"You forgot your change," she said.

He shook his head. "I was wondering about the Help Wanted sign in the window."

"Are you interested?"

The excitement in her voice startled him. "What kind of help do you need?"

Sara glanced toward the kitchen doors, then closed the distance between them. "Let's talk outside." She hustled him out the door and he barely registered the electric shock that skittered across his flesh when she brushed against him.

"I need someone to clean up and make a few repairs so we can list the property."

"You're leaving?"

"I'm trying to convince my father-in-law to move to Albuquerque with me and Dani but this place will never sell in its current condition."

"I could do that."

"José doesn't want to sell. He won't be much help to

you," she warned him. "I can pay ten dollars an hour. I know that's not much but you can stay in the trailer and use the shower in the house. Meals are free."

She hadn't even asked for a reference. *Lucky for you.*

Cruz figured he could spruce up the place and be back on the road in less than a week with a few hundred dollars in his pocket. "That's fine."

Her smile widened but then she suddenly frowned. "You don't carry a gun, do you?"

Unless he wanted to violate his parole and land back in prison, he didn't dare possess a weapon. "No, ma'am. You're welcome to search my truck and my personal belongings."

"I trust you."

She shouldn't.

"I don't like guns." She hugged herself and stared into space, then shook her head. "I'm afraid the trailer doesn't have air-conditioning and most of the windows are broken or missing."

"Not a problem." He'd rather breathe fresh air at night.

"While you settle in, I'll break the news to José." She squared her shoulders. "He won't like you being here, but he doesn't have a say in what I do with my money."

Yet it was José's property. Cruz kept his mouth shut and watched Sara's swinging hips disappear inside the house.

That was the dumbest thing he'd done since he'd been released from prison and considering that he'd only been a free man for a few hours, his future looked more uncertain than ever.

"We don't need help," José grumbled.

Sara removed the clean enchilada pan from his

hands and dried it. She wasn't sure what to make of Cruz Rivera showing up out of the blue asking for work, but she wasn't about to look a gift horse in the mouth. "He's only staying until the property is de-cluttered."

The guarded expression in the new handyman's eyes should have scared Sara away, but she was at her wits' end trying to deal with her stubborn father-in-law. If there was any cause for concern it was *her* reaction to Cruz—just saying his name in her head made her stomach flutter. He was the first man to have her counting back the months since she'd last had sex—seventeen, to be exact.

Cruz was cowboy and bad boy wrapped together in one sexy, dark, dangerous package. She'd noticed him studying her and the appreciative gleam in his brown eyes had contradicted his distant attitude.

"There's nothing wrong with this place." José wasn't a hoarder but after the death of his son, the sixty-five-year-old had grown depressed and had little energy or enthusiasm for chores. As a result, boxes and empty bulk-food containers had piled up. Papago Springs didn't have trash service and the handful of residents either burned their garbage or hauled it to the dump. José hadn't made a trip to the landfill in ages.

When she and Dani had arrived a month ago, she'd had all she could handle cleaning the house, which hadn't seen a dust rag or mop in forever. She'd taken a leave of absence from her pediatric-nurse position at The Children's Center at Presbyterian and she had only four weeks left to convince José to move to Albuquerque before the clinic filled her position.

"Cruz will take the garbage to the dump and tackle what needs fixing before we list with a Realtor."

"I'm not moving."

"Dani and I miss you."

Her father-in-law made an angry noise in his throat but held his tongue. She understood his reluctance to leave. Tony had been his only child and had been born in the house. And José's wife, Sofia, had died here. There were decades of memories within the walls, but that was all that remained—memories. Sara wanted José to make new memories with her and Dani.

Since Tony's death a year and a half ago, Dani could use the extra attention. And it would be such a relief not to have to pay for after-school care or babysitters when Sara worked overtime and weekend shifts at the clinic. With only her income to cover the rent and bills, money was tight. She had Tony's life insurance in case of an emergency, but she didn't want to use any more than she had to, because it was earmarked for Dani's future college tuition. Education had been important to her husband—he'd been the first member of his family to attend college and he'd wanted his daughter to follow in his footsteps.

"You and Dani could move here," José said.

They'd had this discussion before. "I've got a good job in Albuquerque and Dani loves her school." Her daughter had been three and a half when her father died, and although she professed to love him, she didn't really remember him. Tony had spent the majority of his spare time volunteering at the free medical clinic in the barrio. When he'd died, Dani hadn't felt his loss as sharply as Sara had.

"If I leave, who will run the restaurant?" José asked.

She swallowed her frustration. One, maybe two people a week stopped in to eat at the cantina.

"And I can't leave the animals behind," he said.

Animals that other people had asked him to watch while they took *vacations* but then never returned to claim. "We'll find good homes for the mules and the horse." When he remained silent, she said, "What can it hurt to give the place a face-lift whether you move or not?"

"It's a waste of good money."

"It's my money. I'll decide if it's wasted or not."

"How come Antonio never mentioned how stubborn you are?" The corner of José's mouth lifted in a shaky smile.

Sara's heart ached for the old man and she hugged him. He'd been more of a father to her than her own. Her parents had divorced when she'd been a teenager and she'd had no contact with her father since. When Sara had graduated from high school and entered college, her mother met and married a Frenchman, then moved overseas with him. She only saw her mother and stepfather every few years.

"Things will work out, José. You'll see."

José and Dani were all that was left of Sara's *real* family and she was determined to keep them together.

Chapter Two

As far as rusted-out single-wide trailers went, this one was a five-star accommodation compared to where Cruz had laid his head last night. The windowless tin box allowed for plenty of airflow and made the mobile home feel less confining. There were no appliances in the kitchen and only a trickle of rusty water ran out of the faucet when he flipped it on.

Still better than a prison cell.

"My mom says you're gonna help Papa."

The high-pitched little voice startled Cruz. He spun so fast he lost his balance and crashed his hip against the Formica countertop. *Unbelievable*. He'd faced down gangbangers and thugs, yet this pip-squeak had managed to sneak up on him.

He took the stack of clean sheets that were weighing down her arms. "Thank you."

Without waiting for an invitation, Dani walked over to the built-in dinette table and slid onto the bench seat. "My papa doesn't want you to help him."

"Is that right?"

She nodded.

"Why doesn't he want my help?"

Her narrow shoulders moved up and down. Cruz

doubted Sara would approve of him being alone with Dani. "Isn't your mother looking for you?"

Dani's gaze darted to the living room, where a coffee table covered in an inch of dust sat in front of an olive-green sofa. Then her gaze swung back to Cruz and she blurted, "Are you a daddy?"

"No." Several homies in the barrio had gotten their girlfriends pregnant in high school but after seeing how their lives had changed, he'd promised himself that he'd never let a girl trap him with a pregnancy. He'd always carried condoms in his wallet—that is, before he'd landed in jail. He supposed one of the first things he should do when Sara paid him was buy a box of rubbers—in case he ended up in a buckle bunny's bed when he returned to the circuit.

An image of Sara flashed before his eyes. She was the furthest thing from a rodeo groupie and way out of his league. A guy like him wasn't good enough for a widow trying to raise a child on her own.

"A bad man shot my daddy."

"Dani?" José poked his head inside the trailer and glanced between Cruz and his granddaughter. "Did you give Mr. Rivera the sheets?"

Dani nodded.

"Go on, now. Your mama's looking for you," José said.

Dani rolled her eyes and Cruz kept a straight face as she scooted out from behind the table. She stopped in front of him, her big brown gaze beseeching. "If you feed the donkeys, can I help?"

Cruz glanced at José. The suspicious glint in the older man's eyes warned that he wasn't making a social call.

"We'll talk about the donkeys later." José took Dani's hand and helped her down the steps.

Cruz watched the kid scamper across the dirt and duck inside the back of the house. When she was safely out of hearing range, he gave his full attention to Sara's father-in-law.

"I don't want your help," José said.

"Say the word and I'll leave."

Cruz watched the old man struggle—his lips moved but only a harsh breath escaped his mouth, then the fire in his eyes sputtered out. "My daughter-in-law is too trusting." He waved a hand before his face. "Did she ask where you're from?"

"No, sir." Cruz would answer José honestly if he wanted to know, but he wasn't volunteering any information.

"Did she ask where you were going?"

"No, sir."

"Did she ask why you wanted a job?"

"No, sir."

He shook his head. "For all I know, you just got out of prison."

The blood drained from his face, but Cruz held José's gaze.

"I'm keeping an eye on you."

"Yes, sir."

José left, following the path Dani took to the house.

José didn't trust Cruz and he was smart not to. For all intents and purposes, Cruz had lied when he hadn't confirmed José's suspicions about being released from prison. If that wasn't enough incentive to head down the road, then learning that Sara was too trusting of strangers and her husband had been shot should have been. He didn't need trouble and these folks didn't need him.

He grabbed the sheets off the counter, intent on returning them before hitting the road, but a whiff of their clean scent paralyzed him. He buried his face in the cotton and closed his eyes. The sheets smelled like spring, not chlorine and musty body odor. He pictured a room with a queen-size bed covered in the blue flower print. Then he imagined himself sinking onto the mattress and burying his face in a cloud of blond hair.

He set the linens on the counter—it was best if he left without saying goodbye. Tonight he'd sleep in his truck in a parking lot far away from Papago Springs. Halfway to his pickup Sara crossed his path.

"There you are." She offered a smile. "Dani mentioned helping you with the donkeys and that reminded me that I needed to discuss the repairs I'd like you to tackle."

Tell her you changed your mind.

Then she set her hand on his arm and any thought of leaving vanished.

"You aren't afraid of stubborn donkeys, are you?" She smiled.

He would have laughed at her teasing if her fingers hadn't felt like a lit match against his skin.

Chill out. You haven't touched a woman in over a decade. No wonder his testosterone was jumping off the charts. He wanted to believe that any woman he came in contact with would produce the same physical response, but he suspected not. Sara was different from any female he'd known. Pure goodness shone from her eyes, tugging at his protective instincts. And the best way to protect her was to beat it.

"I'd like you to replace the missing slats on the corral, and several windows in the house won't open. And it would be great if you could not only clean up after the animals, but feed them, too."

"I don't think—"

She talked over him. "I'm hoping that once the place is picked up and a Realtor tells my father-in-law what he can get for the property, he'll change his mind about selling. He's all alone now and it's better if he lives with me and Dani in Albuquerque." She spread her arms wide. "But we won't find a buyer for this place in its current condition and I'm afraid I only know how to fix children, not corrals, sheds and fences."

"Fix children?" Her eyes lit up and he wished he'd kept his mouth shut.

"I'm a pediatric nurse."

No wonder José claimed she was too trusting of others. She took care of kids—honest, loving, innocent little people.

"Are you a rodeo cowboy?" She nodded to his worn boots. His twelve-year-old Justin boots had sat in a brown paper bag until he'd reclaimed them earlier today.

"Saddle-bronc rider."

Her eyes twinkled. "Are you any good?"

"Decent."

"I'm sure the things on my list won't take more than a few days to complete. I'll pay you in cash on Friday before you head off to your next rodeo."

"You know much about rodeo?" Why was he encouraging conversation?

"A little. When my husband was in med school, he

got suckered into entering a bull-riding competition by his friends and I got a crash course in emergency medicine." She rubbed the toe of her sandal over a pebble in the dirt. "Antonio died a year and a half ago."

"I'm sorry." For a lot more than Sara would ever know.

"I think the best place to begin would be the corral and the livestock pens. The garbage cans are in the storage shed and the burn barrel is at the back of the property."

Tell her you're leaving.

"The dump is twenty-five miles north, so anything that's too large to burn will have to be taken there." She drew in a breath, then exhaled loudly. "Whether you believe it or not, you're a godsend. I don't know if He sent you—" she pointed at the sky "—or if fate made you stop for a bite to eat. Whatever the reason, you being here will help us all move on."

Dumbfounded, Cruz watched Sara return to the house. How the heck could he walk away from her, Dani and José now? He'd stay—until he cleaned up the property, then he'd get the hell out of Dodge before he did something he'd regret. Like kiss Sara Mendez until the sadness disappeared from her eyes.

"WHAT ARE YOU staring at, Mama?"

Sara jumped back from the window. "Nothing." Her daughter had caught her spying on Cruz—more specifically, admiring the way his snug jeans fit his muscular backside. She could have stood there for hours, watching him work.

"I'm bored."

"Did you finish your work sheets?" Sara had purchased a preschool book for Dani before leaving Albuquerque. Since she'd had to withdraw her from class in order to spend the summer in Papago Springs, she didn't want Dani falling behind the other kids before she entered kindergarten in the fall.

"I don't wanna do work sheets. I wanna help Mr. Cruz feed the donkeys."

Two days had passed since she'd hired Cruz and she'd been amazed and pleased by how much he'd accomplished. The cowboy was up at the crack of dawn and went to work without breakfast, only stopping to eat when she brought him a plate of food.

"You might get in Mr. Cruz's way." This morning he'd removed several broken boards from the corral and replaced them with wood he'd found in the storage shed. Tools and hardware littered the ground and Sara didn't want Dani accidentally cutting herself or stepping on a rusty nail.

"Pleeease…"

"Stop whining, Dani!" Sara rubbed her brow, regretting that she'd snapped at her daughter. She blamed her short temper on José. Every chance he got, her father-in-law grumbled and complained about the work Cruz did. He thought the broken boards gave the corral *character*. Then, when Cruz had removed all the donkey poo from the ground and thrown it in big trash bags to take to the dump, José had grumbled that it was a waste of good manure and should be used for composting. "C'mon." She reached for Dani's hand. "Let's see if there's something Mr. Cruz can find for you to do."

Dani's expression brightened and Sara's heart swelled with love. Tony had been taken from them too early, but she drew strength from her daughter and she credited Dani with helping her move on.

When they stepped outside, Sara shielded her eyes from the midday sun. Keeping hold of Dani's hand, she led her over to the corral, where Cruz worked with his back to them. She stopped short of the tools strewn on the ground and waited until he quit hammering to speak.

"Mr. Cruz," Sara said.

He glanced over his shoulder and Sara sucked in a quiet breath at the way his gaze rolled down her body before returning to her face.

"Is there any chance you might have a chore Dani could help with?"

He crossed the enclosure, stopping in front of them. His shirt was soaked through and for an instant she wished he'd take it off and give her a glimpse of the muscle hiding beneath. The temperature was rising but it hadn't gotten so hot that her mouth should feel like a dry riverbed.

"I'm a good helper," Dani said.

His lips quivered and Sara was disappointed when he didn't smile. She suspected a full-blown grin from him would knock her feet out from under her.

"I found two cans of white paint in the shed. Dani can help paint the corral."

Her daughter tugged on Sara's T-shirt. "I wanna paint. Can I paint? Please can I paint?"

She brushed Dani's bangs out of her eyes. "Go change into the shorts with the tear in the pocket and the T-shirt with the Cheerios box on the front. If you get paint on those clothes, it won't matter."

"Yay!" Dani raced into the house.

"Are you sure she won't be in your way?" Sara studied his face, wondering about his age. The lines etched next to his eyes and his chiseled jaw had her guessing between thirty-five and forty.

"I can't guarantee she'll keep the paint off herself, but if that's okay with you, then I don't mind," he said.

She tore her attention from his face and stared at the pearl snaps on his sweaty cotton shirt, then her gaze dropped to the worn leather belt that hugged his hips.

"I'm collecting a pile of garbage for the dump if you have anything to add to it."

She snapped out of her trance. If he noticed her ogling him, he was too much of a gentleman to mention it. "I'll go through the house and see." There was nothing left to say, but Sara's feet remained firmly planted. If that wasn't perplexing enough, she didn't understand why *he* hadn't gone back to working.

His eyes shifted to the house, then to her, then to the ground before returning to her face. "Dani said her father was shot."

Sara's breath caught in her throat and suddenly the roots on the bottom of her shoes broke off, and she swayed.

"Hey, are you okay?" Cruz grabbed her arm. "Sorry. It's none of my business. I shouldn't have asked."

It took her a moment to find her voice—not because of his question. It wasn't her deceased husband's memory, but Cruz's touch that had rendered her temporarily speechless.

"Antonio volunteered at a free medical clinic in a tough area of Albuquerque. One night while he was closing up, two local gangs got into a shoot-out and a stray bullet came through the window and struck him in the chest. When he hadn't arrived home by ten o'clock,

I called the police, but he was already dead when they arrived."

"I'm sorry."

She cleared her throat. "The next day the police decided it had been a stray bullet from a Los Locos gang member that had killed Tony."

Cruz stiffened. "I better get to work." He disappeared inside the shed, leaving Sara gaping after him.

She made him uncomfortable. All the signs were there—he barely made eye contact. He always took a step back when she approached him. And he answered her questions with as few words as possible. She sensed he was hiding something. But what?

It's none of your concern. Turning off her desire to help others wasn't easy. *Cruz isn't asking for your help.* If there was ever a man who should wear an approach-at-your-own-risk sign around his neck, it was Cruz.

When Sara entered the kitchen, Dani raced past her. "Mind your manners, young lady, and do what Mr. Cruz says."

"I will!" A slamming door punctuated her daughter's exit.

Sara went into the dining room and stood in the shadows near the window facing the corral. She watched Cruz place a can of paint on the ground at Dani's feet. Next, he demonstrated how to dip the brush into the can and wipe off the excess paint. Dani followed his example and whatever he said to her made her beam at him. Cruz might be uncomfortable around Sara but he didn't seem to mind Dani's company.

He carried the second can of paint to another section of fence and worked there. The corral should be torn down but the animals had to be contained somewhere. After a few minutes, Dani set her brush aside, then walked over to Cruz and sat in the dirt. While he worked, she chatted and Sara wished she could hear their conversation. Dani was a friendly child and had inherited her outgoing personality from her father. Antonio had believed helping the needy would make him immune to violence and crime in the barrio. He'd been wrong. Dead wrong.

"Are you lonely, *hija*?"

Sara's father-in-law had an uncanny ability to read her mind. Forcing a smile, she turned from the window. "A little." In truth she was beyond lonely and it had begun long before Antonio had died. Once Dani had been born, her husband had mistakenly believed their daughter would keep Sara so busy she wouldn't notice the long hours he put in at the hospital during the week and then at the clinic on weekends. But Sara had noticed and she'd begged him to spend more time with her and Dani, but her husband had chosen to help strangers over his family.

"He's not the right man for you," José said.

She swallowed a gasp and glanced at the window. "I'm not interested in Mr. Rivera." At least not in a happy-ever-after way. "Why would you think that?"

"Because your eyes follow him everywhere."

This was not a conversation she should be having with her father-in-law. "I want to be sure Dani doesn't make a nuisance of herself."

"And I will make sure you don't bother Mr. Rivera." José turned to leave but Sara stopped him.

"Wait." She didn't want this subject hanging between them when they returned to Albuquerque. There would come a time when she brought a man home, and she didn't want her relationship with José to be adversely affected by that. "Antonio has been dead for over a year and half."

José's stern face crumbled and she rushed to his side, coaxing him to sit in a chair before taking the seat next to him. She didn't have the heart to tell him that the son he'd put on a pedestal all these years had been human and full of faults just like them. "I loved Antonio very much."

"I fell in love with Sofia in high school." He waved a hand in the air. "When she got sick I stayed by her side."

"You were a devoted husband." Sara hadn't been around when Antonio's mother had suffered a stroke and lingered almost a year before passing away.

"Those were hard times, but I never stopped loving her."

"Antonio will always own a piece of my heart, José. But I have to think about Dani's future." At his confused expression she said, "I don't want her to grow up without a father." To be honest Dani didn't know what she was missing since she'd hardly seen her father the first few years of her life. But Sara wanted more for Dani than to be raised by a single mother. Her years working with sick children and their families had proven that kids with two loving parents fared far better facing adversity than those with only one caregiver.

"Dani has me," he said.

"Does that mean you've changed your mind about living with us in Albuquerque?"

He dropped his gaze.

Sara didn't push the subject. "I'm not looking to marry anytime soon, but I do plan to start dating again, if the right man comes along." She resisted the urge to check the window. Cruz Rivera was not the right man, but he was a man who made her pulse race. And he was the first man since Tony's death who made her think of herself—her own needs and yearnings. It was probably best that he clean up the property and leave. Even if José approved of her desire to date again, Cruz was more than she could handle.

"I will think about moving to Albuquerque." José shoved his chair back and shuffled from the room. His footsteps echoed in the hallway that led to the bedrooms at the back of the house. Anytime Antonio came up in conversation, the talk drained José and he retreated to his room.

Sara returned to her post by the window. A good portion of the corral had been painted and it appeared Dani had given up helping, preferring to follow Cruz around and talk his ear off. Her gaze homed in on the handyman. His movements were sure and efficient— he'd have the wooden slats painted in record time. The speed at which he worked had her believing that he couldn't get away from Papago Springs fast enough, which made it all the more interesting that he was still here.

Maybe he has no place to go.

She'd love to learn more about him—where he came from. Where he was headed. If there was a woman in his life.

She knew one thing—he wasn't sticking around because she did his laundry. She'd offered to wash his clothes, but he'd declined.

Maybe he was still here because of the food. José was an amazing cook. Each night she piled Cruz's plate high with food, which he ate in the trailer by himself. And each morning she'd find the previous night's empty plate sitting on the bench by the back door.

It really didn't matter why Cruz was here. It mattered only that with his help she'd be able to convince José to let go of this place. But by then Sara had a sneaking suspicion Cruz Rivera would be long gone.

Chapter Three

Cruz spent Friday afternoon repairing the lean-to for the donkeys and the horse. He'd straightened the once-sagging overhang and set two additional posts in the ground that allowed him to extend the covering, providing more shade for the animals.

"Cruz."

Wiping his sweaty brow across his shirt sleeve he glanced in the direction of Sara's voice. Then he almost swallowed his tongue. She wore a bright turquoise sundress and pretty silver sandals with rhinestones. She'd done something different with her hair—instead of her usual ponytail she wore it loose, the long strands falling over her shoulders in gentle waves.

"I'm taking José into Las Cruces to see his doctor."

"He's not feeling well?"

"He's fine. He has a follow-up appointment to check his blood pressure." She nibbled her lower lip then blurted, "Would you mind if I left Dani here?"

Before he had a chance to object, she rushed on. "It's a long ride and then a long wait in the clinic. Dani's watching a video. She shouldn't be any trouble. She knows to stay in the house and I've put the Closed sign in the front window and locked the door."

"I still have work to do out here." He hoped she'd take the hint that he'd rather not keep an eye on her daughter.

"Dani will be fine in the house. And I made supper. There's a casserole in the fridge. All you have to do is put a serving on a plate and microwave it."

The back door banged open and José stepped outside, wearing a grumpy face. Sara would have her hands full with her father-in-law, so he caved. "Sure. Dani can stay." He'd finish the lean-to then head inside.

"Thank you." She spoke to José. "Ready?"

Cruz couldn't hear what the old man grumbled. Once they drove off, he nailed the final board in place and cleaned up his mess. Toolbox in hand, he entered the house through the back door.

"Dani?"

"Yeah?"

He followed the voice down the hall and poked his head inside the first bedroom. Dani was sprawled across the bed, watching the TV on the dresser.

"I'll be inside the house fixing the windows. Holler if you need me."

"Okay," she said, her gaze glued to the program.

Cruz returned to the kitchen where he'd left José's toolbox and pulled the note paper from his pocket. Yesterday Sara had handed him a list for the house. The windows in her bedroom at the end of the hall needed his attention. He opened the door to the room and the smell of her perfume washed over him. His gaze zeroed in on the bed's bright yellow comforter and sheets. His imagination took off and he dreamed of easing Sara onto the mattress and doing things with her and to her that he had no business thinking. He shifted his attention to the perfume bottles and beauty supplies littering the top of her dresser.

Still he hesitated to enter her private sanctuary, not wanting to contaminate it with his presence.

"What's the matter?"

Cruz glanced down. How long had Dani been standing next to him? Man, the kid was quiet. "I thought you were watching TV?"

She shrugged. "I've seen *Frozen* a hundred times. Have you?"

"No."

"How come you're just standing here?"

He couldn't very well confess that he felt as though he'd violate all that was pure and good about her mother if he entered the room. "I can't remember which window is stuck."

"Both of 'em." Dani squeezed past him, then tried to push the window next to the bed open. She groaned and grunted and her face turned red with effort, then she gave up and crawled onto the bed.

Careful not to touch anything, Cruz crossed the room and set the tool kit on the floor, then tested the window.

"Told you so," Dani said when the window didn't open.

Someone had painted the frame with the window closed and the paint had sealed it shut. Using a flathead screwdriver and a rubber mallet, he chipped away at the paint.

"You're making a mess."

"I know. Can you bring me a dust pan and a broom?"

"What's a dust pan?"

"How about a broom and an old newspaper?"

Dani slid off the bed and left the room. After scraping off the layers of paint, he used his muscle to pry the window open.

"You did it." Dani dragged a small apartment-size vacuum into the room. "My mom uses this to suck stuff up."

"Smart girl."

"I know." She crawled back onto the bed.

When Cruz finished vacuuming the paint chips, he noticed Dani's glum expression. "Do you miss your friends back home?"

"I only have two friends."

That's all Cruz had. Or used to have. Maybe one day he'd look up Alonso and Victor. For now he was leaving his past alone. "What are your friends' names?"

"Tommy and Marissa. We sit together during story time and Tommy always shares his pretzels with me at lunch."

There was something about Dani that relaxed Cruz. Maybe because she was just a child and when she looked at him, she only saw a man trying to help her mother and grandfather. Not a man with a secret.

"Looks like I'm finished here."

"What else are you gonna fix?" she asked.

"That's it for now." He wanted to take a quick shower, then throw in a load of laundry and warm up supper for him and Dani before Sara and José returned.

"Will you play Hi Ho Cherry-O with me?"

"What's that?"

"A game."

"Why don't you set up the game on the kitchen table while I grab a shower."

"Okay." Dani went to her bedroom and Cruz headed

to the trailer for his toiletries and the bag of dirty laundry, then returned to the house.

He showered with his own soap and shampoo. Sara had given him a clean towel at the beginning of the week and he knotted the terry cloth around his waist. Standing in front of the mirror, he studied his face. He didn't know who the man staring back at him was anymore. He recognized the face, but he felt different inside. A huge pit rested at the bottom of his stomach. And it had nothing to do with finally being free. The pit had Sara written all over it—she almost made him forget his promise to Shorty.

After he shrugged into his briefs and jeans, he realized he didn't have a clean T-shirt. He'd have to go bare-chested while he did laundry. He left the bathroom with the duffel and went out to the screened-in porch where the washer and dryer sat. He shoved all his clothes—whites and darks—into the machine, then set the temperature on warm and closed the lid.

"What's that?"

Damn. Cruz knew without asking what Dani was referring to. He should have put on a dirty shirt while he waited for his clothes to finish. He faced the munchkin with pigtails and noticed they were askew. She must have been tugging on them again. "What's what?" he asked, hoping to buy time.

"That picture on your back."

"It's a sun." When he'd turned seventeen, he'd had the ancient Zia sun symbol used on the New Mexico flag tattooed on the back of his shoulder. A capital *L* had been etched into his skin above the symbol and below it—for the name of the gang he'd been trying to pledge. At the time he hadn't known a school teacher would throw a wrench in his plans and he'd never complete his gang initiation.

"It's not a very pretty sun."

"You're right. I should have it taken off."

"Can I see it again?" she asked.

Sara and José wouldn't be pleased with Dani's interest in the tattoo, but maybe if he didn't make a big deal of it, she wouldn't blab to her mother. He crouched down.

"How come there's two letter *L*s?"

"It's the letter of my mother's and grandmother's names," he lied.

"What's their names?"

"Lina and Lolita." Time to change the subject. He didn't want to think about his family, who'd written him off when he'd gone to prison. "Are you hungry?"

She nodded.

"Let's find out what your mother made for supper." He followed Dani into the kitchen where she opened the refrigerator.

"What is it?" Her big brown eyes blinked.

"A casserole."

"What kind?"

"I don't know." After scooping a spoonful onto a plate, he put it in the microwave. While the food warmed he poured Dani a glass of milk and got out silverware. When he set the meal on the kitchen table next to the board game, he said, "Blow on it first so you don't burn your tongue."

She climbed onto the chair and pushed the food around on her plate. "It's crazy noodle casserole," she said. "It's got a bunch of different noodles in it and spaghetti sauce and cheese."

"I like spaghetti sauce." He put a second plate with a bigger serving into the microwave for himself.

Dani slurped her milk. "How did you know I like milk?"

"Don't most kids like milk?"

She nodded.

He brought his plate to the table and joined her. He was uncomfortable sitting at the table without a shirt. When he heard the washer stop, he said, "Be right back." He put a single T-shirt into the dryer, then, after a few minutes, took it out and tugged the damp material over his head before tossing the rest of the load into the dryer. When he returned to the table Dani had finished her meal.

"You want seconds?" he asked.

"I want cake."

"Did your mother bake a cake?"

"Papa did."

"What kind?"

"Chocolate. I helped frost it."

A sharp pain caught Cruz in the chest. Chocolate cake had been his younger brother's favorite. Their mother had stopped baking cakes after Emilio had been killed in a drive-by shooting. "What do you say we wash our dishes first, then I'll cut you a piece of cake?"

Dani slid off the chair and carried her dish to the sink. "Are you gonna have a piece, too?"

"I'm full from supper. I'll have one later." He set his dishes in the sink, too. "Do you want to wash or dry?"

"Dry."

Cruz moved a chair closer to the counter and lifted Dani onto the seat. "Where's the dish soap?"

"In there." She pointed to the cabinet below the sink.

"Dishcloth?"

"Papa uses this." She handed him the scrub brush already sitting in the sink and he cleaned a plate and rinsed it. "I guess you need a towel."

Dani pointed to the drawer next to his hip.

He handed her a towel and they worked side by side.

"My daddy never washed dishes."

"Guys don't like to do dishes."

"Papa does dishes." She dried off a plate and placed it next to her on the counter.

"You're lucky to have a papa." The only extended family Cruz had been in contact with growing up had been his paternal grandmother and she'd died when he turned twelve. Probably a good thing, because she would have been disappointed that Cruz had followed in his father's footsteps and landed in prison—no matter that he'd taken the fall for his friend.

A horn beeped, alerting Cruz that Sara and José had returned.

"Mama's home!" Dani jumped down from the chair and raced outside.

Cruz made quick work of finishing the dishes and wiping off the countertops.

"Thanks for cleaning up," Sara said when she entered the kitchen and spotted the dish rag in his hand.

"Thanks for supper." He nodded to the fridge. "Dani hasn't had dessert yet."

"Would you like a piece of cake?" She dropped her purse on the table.

"No, thanks. I'll grab my laundry and get out of your way." He scooted past her, holding his breath so he wouldn't inhale her perfume. On the porch he stuffed his still damp clothes into his bag and left. He spotted

Dani and José at the corral but ducked inside the trailer before either of them noticed him.

He spent the next ten minutes spreading his damp jeans across the counter and kitchen table, then he hung his T-shirts in the closet and left the door open. Without air-conditioning they'd be dry in no time.

Restless, he paced across the room. When José and Dani went back into the house, he'd sit on the trailer steps and enjoy the night air. He didn't mind sleeping in the single-wide—it was bigger than his prison cell—but the tin box didn't cool off until after the sun went down. It wasn't until he sat on the sofa that he noticed the three one-hundred-dollar bills along with a note on the table.

Thanks for all your help this week. Hope it's enough to cover your entry fee wherever you rodeo tomorrow. Sara.

The money was more than enough, but Cruz didn't want to rodeo. Yeah, he'd promised Shorty he'd hit the circuit and he was determined to make good on that vow, but not yet. He hadn't pictured himself as a handyman, but the hard work this week had been therapeutic and had kept him from thinking about his time in prison and why he'd ended up there. He'd never be able to ward off the memories during a long drive to a rodeo.

Memories of his buddies Alonso and Victor. A part of him yearned to reconnect with the guys. But he wasn't sure he could handle seeing them, especially Victor. Cruz was still pissed that he'd followed Vic to Salvador Castro's house. If Cruz had let Vic go by himself to confront the gang leader, he wouldn't have ended up in prison. But Vic wouldn't back down and their friendship demanded that Cruz be his wingman. Vic had wanted Salvador to take responsibility for getting Vic's sister pregnant. Threats and insults were exchanged at the Five Points intersection in downtown Albuquerque. When Vic had pulled a gun from beneath his jacket, no one had been more surprised than Cruz. Fearing his friend would take things too far, Cruz wrestled the gun from Vic's hand, but then the weapon had discharged accidentally, the bullet hitting Salvador in the shoulder.

The police arrived and Cruz was put into the backseat of a patrol car and whisked away.

What's done is done.

Yeah, there was nothing he could do to change the past. He could only move forward. And he would. Eventually. He'd finished everything on Sara's to-do list, but he didn't want to leave her, José or Dani. Not yet.

He'd been in Papago Springs less than a week but already Sara's kindness, Dani's chatter and even José's moodiness had begun to fill the hollow feeling he'd carried in his gut for longer than he could remember. Each day the lost feeling inside him shrunk a little. For now he was right where he needed to be—safe from the outside world, sleeping like a baby at night.

Tomorrow he'd find a chore that needed doing, so he'd have an excuse not to rodeo.

SARA WOKE AT the crack of dawn Saturday morning worried Cruz would take off without saying goodbye. He'd been a huge help in cleaning up the property and the three hundred dollars' pay was hardly much money, but the man could eat—oh, could he eat. Their grocery bill for the week had skyrocketed. José was an incredible cook, but good grief, Cruz acted as if he'd been deprived of decent food for years.

As soon as the coffeepot stopped dripping, she filled a foam cup with the hot brew and put a plastic lid on it so Cruz could take it on the road with him. She left the house certain she'd find him packing his belongings in the back of his pickup. In the four days he'd been in Papago Springs, she'd learned very little about him. She admitted she was nosy and wanted to know where he'd grown up. Did he have family? A girlfriend? A child from a previous marriage?

Does it matter?

No, she supposed not, but feminine curiosity had gotten the best of her and she secretly wanted him to stick around longer. So did Dani. Last night when she'd tucked her daughter into bed, Dani had chatted about her and Cruz doing the dishes together and how he'd promised to play a board game with her but Sara and José had come home and interrupted them.

Cruz's truck still sat parked at the side of the house, so Sara veered off toward the trailer. She knocked softly on the door. No answer. She poked her head inside. "Cruz? Are you up?" Silence. The faint sound of hammering echoed in the air and she headed to the dilapidated barn across the property. There were gaping holes in the structure and part of the roof had caved in a decade ago.

When she entered the structure, she stopped in her tracks and stared at Cruz's shirtless, glistening bare torso as he sorted through lumber. With each board he tossed onto a nearby pile, his biceps bunched and his pecs winked at her. She swallowed hard when desire gripped her gut. The hot sensation spread through her limbs, leaving her weak and trembling.

He must have sensed her scrutiny, because he froze, his arms above his head, a board balanced in his hands. His gaze collided with hers and no matter how she tried to shift her attention to his face, her eyeballs remained glued to his dark nipples and hairless chest.

Too bad rodeo cowboys didn't ride without their shirts on—she just might give up nursing and become a buckle bunny.

Someone had to speak. "What are you doing?" she asked.

"Sorting through the wood pile." He dropped the piece in his hands, then removed his work gloves and wiped his sweaty brow. He stared at his T-shirt a few feet away but made no move to put it on.

"I thought you were rodeoing today." She lifted the cup. "I made your coffee to go."

"I decided not to." He stepped forward and took the drink. "Thanks."

"Why the change of heart?"

He ignored her question and waved at the wood pile. "I noticed the boards earlier in the week. Most of them are in decent shape. You should be able to get some money for them."

"I appreciate the thought, but…"

"If you want, I can leave."

She didn't want him to leave. The thought of never seeing him again had kept her up all night. Her mind scrambled for a way to keep him with her a little while longer. "I'm driving into Las Cruces later to meet with a Realtor." She shrugged. "I didn't want to do it yesterday because it would have only upset José. You're welcome to come with me and while we're in town we could check into selling that wood at the lumberyard."

"Sure. I'll load the boards in my truck."

"How long do you need?"

"An hour."

"Okay." She left the barn and rushed back to the house, where she fussed with her hair and makeup, then spent the next few minutes staring at the clothes in her closet. She needed to look respectable and business-like for her appointment with the Realtor, but today's temperature would be in the nineties. She settled on a pair of khaki linen pants and a colorful tank top. Maybe after the appointment she could convince Cruz to stop for lunch before they returned to Papago Springs.

"Where are you going dressed like that?" José asked when he almost plowed Sara over in the hallway.

"I have a few errands to run in Las Cruces."

"We were just there. How come you didn't pick up what you needed then?"

"I forgot." She hoped her father-in-law couldn't tell she was lying. "Cruz is going with me and we're taking the old wood in the barn along to see if we can sell it at the lumberyard."

"What if I need the wood to fix something?"

He hadn't fixed anything on the property in eons.

"Can you think of any groceries that you need?"

"Milk for Dani."

"I'll take the cooler, then." She retrieved the ice chest from the porch and set it outside by Cruz's truck. "If Dani gives you any trouble today, she can do her work sheets."

"You make her study too much. Let her enjoy her childhood." José was stuck in a time warp in Papago Springs. He had no clue what went on in the world and how important it was for children to be prepared before they entered kindergarten.

"The work sheets are fun and keep her busy. There's nothing wrong with exercising the brain."

José made a growling sound in his throat and walked into the kitchen.

"I'll call if we won't be home for supper." She hurried outside before José protested. She understood that he was suspicious of Cruz because they knew so little about him. But from the moment Sara had looked into his brown eyes, instinct had kicked in and she knew he was trustworthy and meant them no harm. Years of being a nurse and questioning parents when they brought their sick or injured children to the clinic had taught her to read between the lines and decipher facial expressions and body language. She could spot a liar before they opened their mouth to speak.

Too bad Antonio hadn't listened to her when she'd insisted he quit working at the clinic in the barrio because it wasn't safe. The night he'd been killed he'd called her before leaving the hospital to head to the clinic and she'd asked him not to go. She'd had a bad feeling that something would happen. And it had—Antonio had ended up dead.

She always trusted her gut—it had never let her down. By the end of the day she'd know a lot more about Cruz and could put José's worries to rest.

Chapter Four

"I'll wait here," Cruz said when he parked outside the realty office located in a strip mall in Las Cruces.

"Are you sure? I wouldn't mind having someone else listen to the Realtor in case I forget what he says."

Cruz nodded to the pay phone outside the grocery store across the lot. "I need to make a call."

She frowned. "You don't have a cell phone?"

"Nope." And he doubted he'd be able to afford one anytime soon.

"I admire you for snubbing your nose at technology. I'd give anything to fall off the grid for a month or two—" if Sara knew just how far he'd fallen off the grid in the past twelve years, she'd be shocked "—but I'm required to carry a phone with me at all times in case there's an emergency at the clinic." She hopped out of the truck. "I won't be too long."

Cruz weaved between the parked cars and entered the grocery store, where he purchased a calling card with sixty minutes of talk time. He returned outside and retrieved his parole officer's contact information from his pocket, then swiped the calling card and entered the number.

"Ed Kline."

"Cruz Rivera."

"You were supposed to call four days ago. Where are you?"

The sound of shuffling papers echoed in Cruz's ear.

"Papago Springs."

"I've heard of it. Not much of a town."

"I landed a temporary job there."

"Doing what?"

"Handyman work."

"I'll need the name of your employer and a contact number."

"Sure." Cruz would be long gone by the time the parole officer got around to phoning José. "Sofia's Mexican Cantina. Highway 26, Papago Springs. José Mendez owns the restaurant."

"Phone number?"

Cruz rattled off the number.

"How long do you plan to work there?"

"Not sure."

"Do you have a place to live?"

"The restaurant owner is letting me bunk down in a trailer on the property."

"Are you paying rent?"

"No."

Silence followed the inquisition. "Look, Rivera. It's my job to see that you integrate back into society the right way. That means finding a job where you fill out employment forms, pay taxes and a place to live where you pay rent. You also need to sign up for health care."

"I don't need health insurance." After being told what to do 24/7 for so long, Cruz didn't care to play by someone else's rules.

"What about rodeo? You plan to do any of that in the future?"

The parole officer was aware of Cruz's prison rodeo career and before he'd been released, Kline had encouraged Cruz to continue to compete. Everyone assumed he was full of rage and anger and that busting broncs would help keep his violent emotions in check. But twelve years was a long time to hold on to one's anger and any wrath he'd felt when he'd been handed down his sentence had been sucked out of him long ago. He was too tired and too hollow inside to care about getting even or seeking revenge.

Being around Sara, Dani and José had reinforced his desire to put the past behind him and move forward one step at a time. "I might rodeo."

"Let me know if you do. Have you contacted anyone in your family?"

"No." A year ago he'd received the news that his mother had passed away after a sudden heart attack. With his father still in prison, the only family he had left was a sister and a brother a few years younger than him—both sired by different men. He'd lost contact with his siblings after he'd entered prison and he doubted they cared one way or the other that he was a free man.

"If and when you purchase a vehicle I'll need the VIN number, make and model and your driver's license."

His fingers clamped tighter on the receiver. "Yeah, sure."

"And I need to know when you leave Papago Springs."

"I understand."

"You haven't purchased a firearm, have you?"

"No."

"No drug use and go easy on the alcohol."

Cruz clenched his teeth together, hating that Kline spoke to him like a child.

"That's it for now. Keep your nose clean. I'll try to pay you a visit in the next month."

"Sure." Cruz wasn't worried. Parole officers were overworked. As soon as he hung up, Kline would forget him. He disconnected the call and returned to the truck. A short while later Sara emerged from the realty office. She didn't look happy.

"Everything okay?" he asked when she slid onto the passenger seat.

"José's restaurant is worth just about nothing. The Realtor said we'll be lucky if we sell the property in the next five years."

That didn't sound good. He started the engine and flipped on the air.

"The land is worth more than the restaurant business and for the right price, he said, we might be able to lease the property to someone looking for a place to board horses."

"What does that mean for convincing José to move to Albuquerque with you?" Cruz asked.

"Not sure, but closing the restaurant, then leasing the land and barn might be our best option. If things work out and José doesn't mind living with Dani and me, then he can sell the place if and when a buyer comes along."

"Sounds like a plan."

"There's only one problem," she said.

"What's that?"

"Would you be willing to stick around and make the necessary repairs to the barn?"

Panic shot through Cruz and he squeezed the steering wheel.

"I trust you to do a good job and even if we need to hire a professional construction company to help you, I'd like you to supervise the work to make sure José isn't overcharged."

The word *trust* echoed in Cruz's ear. If he stayed in Papago Springs, his parole officer would eventually call José and then his secret would be no longer. A part of him wanted to leave before Sara found out about his past. He'd rather have her remember him as a good man and not a down-on-his-luck parolee. But what kind of man would leave a woman in a lurch—not a man he wanted to be.

"I can pay you more," she said. "I've managed to put aside some savings for a rainy day."

Depleting her rainy-day fund didn't sit well with Cruz. He'd work for free—it was the least he could do since Tony had been shot by the gang he'd once wanted to be a part of.

"I'll work on the barn in exchange for room and board." It would cost her plenty just to feed him and purchase supplies.

"Fine." Her chin jutted. "But I'm paying for your gas each time you make a trip to the lumberyard in Las Cruces."

He didn't want her filling his tank, but he admired her pride. If Sara was determined to coax José to leave Papago Springs, he'd do what he could to help the family remain together. "I'll stay."

Sara's eyes flashed with gratitude and a caution flag

waved inside his brain, warning him to keep his distance. It would be too easy to mistake gratitude for attraction. "While we grab lunch, we can compile a list of supplies before we stop at the lumberyard on the way out of town," she said.

"Name the restaurant."

"There's a diner that serves great malts. The burgers are decent, too."

He shifted into Drive and left the shopping center. Worry gnawed at his gut. The last occasion that he'd tried to help someone out, he'd ended up in jail. He sure in hell hoped this time would be different.

"YOU'RE WASTING GOOD money, daughter."

José peered over Sara's shoulder as she stood in the kitchen looking out the sliding glass door at the barn. Almost a week had passed since she and Cruz had returned from their trip into Las Cruces. She'd informed José about her chat with the Realtor, then laid out in detail her idea to repair the barn and lease the property, hoping that leasing and not selling would put her father-in-law at ease. He'd agreed with the plan—thank goodness—insisting he'd move in with her and Dani for a year before deciding to remain in Albuquerque or return to Papago Springs. After the improvements Cruz had made to the property, she sensed José was getting cold feet even though no customers—zero—had stopped at the restaurant the past few days.

"Once the place is fixed up, we'll advertise in the Las Cruces paper and post flyers around the town. Horse owners will jump at the opportunity to lease the barn and the twenty-five acres behind it." She hoped.

José opened his mouth to object but she cut him off. "Would you check on Dani?"

After he left the room, she grabbed a cold jug of water from the fridge and crossed the yard to where Cruz hammered boards over a gaping hole in the side of the barn. The temperature hovered near ninety and his T-shirt was soaked with sweat. He should shuck the shirt and be done with it.

You'd like that, wouldn't you?

Yes, she would. She hadn't thought about her sex life in a very long time but when she stared at Cruz's handsome face, a tingling sensation spread through her body, making her yearn for that special intimacy between a man and a woman—not that sex with Tony had been *special* after Dani had been born. Her husband had thrown himself into his job and volunteer work—if he'd gotten five hours of sleep a night he'd been lucky. When they did set aside time for each other in the bedroom, the experience was short-lived. Tony used up all his energy doctoring others and there had been little left over for her.

Cruz must have sensed her presence because he glanced over his shoulder, then stiffened when he spotted her. She wasn't all that experienced with men— there had only been one other before Tony. Still, she didn't need experience to read between the lines. She and Cruz were attracted to each other. He was a man of few words and probably a whole lot of secrets. But that was okay with her, because he wasn't hanging around forever—so what could it hurt if they stole a few moments of excitement for themselves?

He broke eye contact and walked into the barn. She smiled at the thought that she unnerved him. She was feeling brazen today, so she followed him. When she entered the barn she found Cruz struggling to nail a two-by-four in place across the door of a stall. She set down the water and rushed to help.

"Thanks," he grunted, the protruding nails in his mouth wiggling. He secured one end of the board, then inched toward her. She caught a whiff of soap and hard-working male. "I've got it now." His brown eyes bored into hers and she froze, hypnotized by the shimmering color.

She stepped out of the way.

He wiped a damp sleeve across his face. "How does José feel about you helping me?"

"I don't know. And I don't care." She tore her gaze from his sweaty face and nodded to the jug. "I brought cold water."

"Thanks." He stepped past her and reached for the jug. He guzzled the water, the liquid spilling from his mouth and running down his chin. When he finished he said, "It's been quiet around here. Who else lives in town?"

"Charlie DuPont owns the empty strip mall across the street. He lives in an apartment above the beauty shop. Charlie's a recluse. Every morning he signals that he's okay by raising the window shade."

"Who owns the empty gas station?"

"Leroy Hansen. He lives in a mobile home two miles west of here. Brings his wife, Betty, in for dinner at the restaurant once a month. And the Conrads live next door, but they separated a year ago and Sheila moved out. Mike comes around to check on the place once in a while, but he's got a girlfriend in Las Cruces and stays with her."

"It's just José and Charlie that live in town, then?" Cruz asked.

"Doug Andrews owns the bar but it's only open during the winter months. He spends the rest of the year at his cabin in Colorado." She shrugged. "That's why I want José to leave. If he ever gets injured or suffers a stroke or something, there'd be no one to help him."

"What happens to Charlie if José leaves?"

Sara wondered why Cruz was so talkative today but she wasn't about to question his chattiness for fear he'd clam up. "I have Charlie's daughter's phone number. If José leaves, Jill and her husband will come get Charlie." She nodded to the wood pile behind him. "I'm free to help you this afternoon." Was it her imagination or did Cruz's eyes darken as he stared at her? Her gaze dropped to his chest where she swore his pounding heart made the damp cotton move in rhythm to her own thudding heart. "I think we should just get it over with," she blurted.

"Get what over with?"

She inched closer and the distance between them vanished. Then she rose on tiptoe and pressed her mouth to his. She felt his quick intake of breath and expected him to pull away. He didn't. Her senses went on high alert and she closed her eyes, absorbing the feel of his lips beneath hers. The breath he'd sucked in moments before puffed against her face in a gentle whisper of air.

"Mama?"

Sara jumped. Cruz spun so fast she teetered sideways and he grabbed her arm to keep her from stumbling. "In here, Dani!" she called out.

"I can't see." Dani stopped in the shadows.

"I'm right here, honey." Sara walked toward her daughter. "It takes a minute for your eyes to adjust after being in the bright sunlight." She whisked her daughter's hair off her forehead. Heart still racing from a kiss that never got off the ground, she said, "You need your bangs trimmed."

Dani peeked around Sara. "Can I help Mr. Cruz?"

"I told Papa to have you do your work sheets."

"I hate work sheets. I wanna help Mr. Cruz."

Sara heard the longing in her daughter's voice. Dani wasn't just bored; she wanted attention—Cruz's attention. José smothered Dani with affection and love but he was her papa. Sara was certain Dani viewed Cruz in a different light—most likely as a father figure.

"She can stay."

Sara couldn't read Cruz's expression and Dani didn't wait for her mother to decide before she ran through the barn, skidding to a stop at the stall Cruz was repairing. "I can help you paint."

"We don't need to paint this time," he said. "Once I nail this board into place, you can sweep out the stall."

"Okay. I'll get a broom." Dani raced off.

"I can find something for her to do," Sara said.

"She'll be fine." He cleared his throat. "Unless you don't want her helping me."

Why would he think she'd object to Dani being with him? There it was again—a tiny shiver that warned her Cruz was hiding something. Even though intuition said there was a lot more to Cruz than just a cowboy passing through town, Sara didn't feel threatened by him.

"I gotta broom," Dani said when she returned.

"You stand back for a minute and let me nail this board in place."

"Papa says it's stupid to fix the barn, but I think the donkeys are gonna like their new home."

"You're right. The animals will appreciate a clean place to rest when it's cold outside."

Forgotten by Cruz and Dani, Sara returned to the house. She'd hardly be a good mother if she was jealous of her daughter. Even so, she couldn't help being a little envious of a five-year-old.

"Aren't you going to stay out there with Dani?" José stood in the doorway, blocking her entrance.

"Why? Dani's not afraid of Cruz."

"She should be."

Sara pushed past her father-in-law and stopped in the kitchen. "Why should Dani be afraid of him? Do you know something I don't?"

"A man just called, wanting to speak to me about Cruz." José held out a piece of note paper.

"'Ed Kline,'" Sara read the name out loud. "What did he want?"

The lines bracketing José's mouth deepened. "He's a parole officer."

The blood drained from Sara's face and her gaze shot back to the barn.

"Cruz Rivera just got out of prison."

"What did the parole officer want?"

"He wanted to make sure I gave permission for Cruz to stay on the property."

"What else did he ask?"

"If I was employing Cruz. I said yes."

"And?"

"And I'm to call him right away when Cruz leaves."

Sara nibbled her lower lip. Dani was sweeping horse

stalls with an ex-con. Darn it, she'd had a feeling Cruz was hiding something.

"Tell him to go," José said. "I don't want my granddaughter near a man who's been in prison."

"I'm a pretty good judge of character," she said. "If I thought for one moment that Dani was in danger I'd ask Cruz to leave."

"Sara."

"What?"

"Cruz Rivera was in prison for attempted manslaughter."

Manslaughter?

"What happened?"

"I didn't ask and the parole officer didn't volunteer the information."

"What else did you learn?" she asked.

"Rivera was the prison's shining rodeo star. He set records in bronc busting."

Sara rubbed her brow. She seriously hadn't given a thought to where Cruz had come from when he'd shown up two weeks ago. Never in her wildest imagination would she have pegged him for an ex-con. Her protective instincts kicked in, and she said, "I better fetch Dani."

"Are you going to tell him to leave?"

Hand on the door, she froze. Cruz was working for room and board. If she kicked him to the curb, she'd have to pay a huge sum of money to a contractor to finish the repairs to the barn. "Once he finishes working on the barn I'll tell him he has to move on."

"And what about you?"

She forced herself to make eye contact with her father-in-law. "What about me…what?"

"Are you going to let him go?"

Evidently she hadn't hidden her attraction to Cruz very well. "There's nothing going on between me and Cruz."

"Yet."

"I can take care of myself." She'd been doing as much the entire time she'd been married to his son.

"You admitted you're lonely."

She looked away.

"The first few years are the hardest." José's eyes glazed over as if he were going back in time to when Sofia had died. "You come into the house expecting to hear their voice, but only silence greets you. So you talk out loud, thinking they can hear and tell you what to do. Then you dream about them. Night after night you beg them to come to back, only to wake up in the morning alone in bed." He shook his head and stared at Sara. "You're young. You shouldn't live the rest of your life alone, but Tony would not approve of Rivera. He would want a better man to help raise his Dani."

Seriously? Tony wouldn't care who raised his daughter.

As soon as the thought entered her mind, Sara felt ashamed. Just because Tony had chosen his career over his family didn't mean he hadn't cared about them or hadn't loved them as best he could. Still…there was something about Cruz Rivera that didn't jive with a manslaughter charge.

"You don't have to worry about me or Dani, José. Cruz is only here to help us before he moves on." She left the house and made a beeline for the barn, stopping inside the doorway. She didn't see Dani or Cruz. In a moment of panic her heart stopped beating, then she silently cursed José for putting bad thoughts about Cruz into her head.

She heard voices coming from the storage room. When she reached the back of the barn, she eavesdropped.

"Mama said my daddy was a good doctor and he helped lots of people," Dani said.

"Helping people is important."

That didn't sound like something a hardened criminal would say.

"Do you help people?" Dani asked.

"Sometimes. I'm helping your papa by fixing his barn." After a moment of silence he said, "And I helped a friend once, but that didn't work out as I'd planned."

"Huh?"

"Never mind. Can you hold this bucket while I look for another box of nails?"

"Are you gonna go home with me and my mom?"

"Dani?" Sara stepped through the doorway. "Papa wants you."

"But I'm helping Mr. Cruz."

Cruz's gaze collided with Sara's and he frowned. "That's okay, Dani. I'll find the nails."

Dani looked beseechingly at Sara. "Can I help Mr. Cruz later?"

"We'll see." She set her hands on Dani's shoulders and gave her a gentle nudge toward the exit. "Go on."

Once Dani left, Cruz asked, "What's wrong?"

"Nothing, why?"

He shook his head. "You look nervous."

"I do?" Her smile trembled.

His eyes were a turbulent swirl of brown and black. "You know, don't you?"

Chapter Five

Sara swallowed hard. "Your parole officer called José."

Cruz closed his eyes and silently let loose a string of cuss words. He'd known all along Papago Springs was a temporary pit stop before he hit the rodeo circuit. But somewhere in the past two weeks he'd dropped his guard and had gotten caught in a fantasy of belonging here with Sara, Dani and José.

But you don't belong with them.

No kidding. He opened his eyes and winced at the uncertainty reflected in Sara's blue gaze. "I'll pack my things and be gone in an hour." He made a move to step past her, but her fingers clamped down on his arm and he froze. The warmth from her touch spread through his muscles and he fisted his hands to keep from pulling her close. He ached to kiss her—really kiss her—before he left. He wanted to take the taste and feel of her lips with him.

"Did you try to kill the person or was it an accident?" she whispered.

He looked her straight in the eye. "It was an accident."

She studied him for the longest time and the indecision in her gaze hurt more than he wanted to admit.

Then she took a deep breath and exhaled loudly. "I believe you."

His knees went weak with relief. He barely knew Sara, yet it mattered a heck of a lot that she believed he hadn't meant to shoot a man. "Thanks."

He pulled free of her hold and headed for the exit.

"Where are you going?"

He stopped. "To pack my things."

"Stay."

He swallowed hard at her soft plea, savoring the feeling of rightness that filled him. "It's better if I go." José would want him gone.

"I didn't peg you for a man who left people in a lurch."

She knew him better than he knew himself. If he'd let Victor go alone instead of tagging along, he wouldn't be standing here right now.

And you never would have met Sara.

"It's better if I go."

"Better for whom?"

"You." Then he added, "And Dani and José."

"All I'm asking is for you to stay until the barn is repaired. Then you can…take off."

That was the problem. He had nowhere to go once he left Papago Springs.

"Please. If you don't help me, I'll never convince José to leave this one-horse town and move to Albuquerque."

He wanted to stay—more than anything. But this wasn't Sara's property and she didn't have the final say. He left the barn, aware of her eyes burning a hole in his back as he walked to the house. He knocked on the back door and when José appeared, he said, "I need to talk to you."

José nodded and turned away so Cruz took that as an invitation to enter. He stepped into the kitchen but remained by the door. José returned to the stove where he was frying fajita meat.

"Sara said my parole officer called you." He wished the old man would look at him. He hated talking to the back of his head. "I did twelve years for attempted manslaughter."

"Are you guilty?" José asked.

"The gun went off by accident and I was holding it, so yeah, I guess I was guilty."

A quick glance over his shoulder was all José offered as acknowledgment that he'd heard the confession. "I'll leave if you want me to," Cruz said.

José's shoulders slumped. "I think you should go—" Cruz spun toward the door "—but my daughter-in-law wants you to stay."

Clutching the handle, Cruz waited for him to continue. When only silence filled the room, he faced the old man.

"You don't have the eyes of a killer," José said. "You can stay until the barn is finished, but then you go. And when you go, you don't take Sara or Dani with you."

José was afraid Cruz would woo his daughter-in-law and granddaughter away and he'd be left alone. He wanted to reassure him that he had no intention of letting anything happen between Sara and him. "I'm not the right man for Sara. She deserves better."

"Good. We agree on that."

"Did Kline want me to call him?"

"No. He wants me to call him when you leave."

Cruz nodded. "I better get back to work."

"One more thing," José said.

"What?"

"Don't hurt Sara or Dani."

"I would never—"

"I'm not talking about that kind of hurt. I'm telling you not to break their hearts."

"I'll keep my distance." He'd try to, anyway.

"Hi, Mr. Cruz." Dani walked into the kitchen, carrying a doll in one hand and its head in the other. "Can you fix her?" She held up the toy. "Misty's head keeps falling off."

Cruz glanced at José, but he'd already turned back to the stove. "Let me try." He used a little muscle to attach the doll head to the body. "There you go."

"Thanks. Wanna come to our tea party?"

Cruz caught the way José's body went rigid. "No, thanks. I have work to do." He slipped out the door and returned to the barn where Sara waited for him.

"Well?" she asked.

"I'm staying. Until the barn is repaired."

"Thank you."

She should thank José for allowing him to remain on the property. She touched his arm and he quickly stepped out of reach. "What's wrong?"

Now that he knew for certain Sara was off-limits, touching was forbidden. Before his past had caught up with him, he could at least pretend they had a chance at a budding romance—now there would be no more pretending.

"It's best if you keep Dani out of my way."

She frowned. "Did José tell you to stay away from her?"

"In so many words. You, too." He went into the storage room, pretending he needed something in there—anything to put distance between him and Sara.

"I'm a grown woman, Cruz. I can make decisions for myself and my daughter even if my father-in-law can't accept that."

Her words did nothing to reassure him. All he had to do was look at her. Smell her. Touch her. And his testosterone spiked. But there was no way he'd come between Sara and José. Family was important—he had no idea how he'd come to that conclusion when his own family had fallen by the wayside years ago.

Your father still cares.

The last time Cruz had seen his father had been right before his world had caved in on him. Riley Fitzgerald had flown Cruz to the South Dakota State Penitentiary in Sioux Falls so he could visit his old man. What would Sara think if she knew he'd followed in his father's footsteps—the only difference being that the man Cruz had shot had survived and the one who'd fallen on his father's knife hadn't? T.C. Rivera still had ten years left on his sentence. Who the heck knew if there would be anything remaining of the father he'd once known after he got out.

"I should be finished with the repairs next week," he said. When she didn't respond, he looked over his shoulder and discovered he was alone in the barn. Sara had spunk and determination, but from now on he'd do his admiring of her from afar. Suddenly Saturday's rodeo in Alamogordo was looking better and better. It wouldn't hurt to get out of Papago Springs for a while and he was pretty sure José wouldn't mind him disappearing for a day.

"ARE YOU SURE you don't want to come to the rodeo with us?" Sara asked José early Saturday morning.

She flipped the pancakes on the griddle, then went in search of the maple syrup.

"Leroy and Betty are coming in for dinner tonight."

Sara forgot that the couple made a trip into Papago Springs once a month to socialize with José. "I'm sure they'd understand if you canceled on them."

"Too late now. I made the enchilada sauce last night."

He was lying, but she didn't call him on it. Truth be told, she was looking forward to her and Dani spending the day with Cruz. It would be a relief to not have her every move around him watched and analyzed by her father-in-law. And Dani was excited to go to her first rodeo.

"I have no idea when we'll be home but I'll call you after we leave the fairgrounds." If Cruz had been shocked that she'd invited herself and Dani along with him for the day, he'd hid it well.

The sooner they left the better, because she didn't expect José's mood to improve. She slid the pancakes onto a platter, then left the kitchen to check on Dani's progress. When she opened the door she found the room empty and the outfit she'd left out for Dani to wear missing from the chair.

Sara bypassed the kitchen and went outside through the front door where she discovered Dani sitting on the hood of Cruz's truck, chatting his ear off.

"Mama, Mr. Cruz said he's gonna ride a horse today but not the bulls 'cause the bulls are big and mean."

"Is that right?" Sara couldn't take her eyes off Cruz. He looked *h-o-t* in his brand-new jeans and Western pearl-snap shirt. Then her gaze dropped lower and she caught sight of his belt buckle. She nodded to the silver. "That looks like a bull, not a horse."

"The buckle belonged to my father. My mother sent it to me years ago."

Amazing that the buckle hadn't gone missing while he'd been in prison. "Is it real?"

"Yep. Championship buckle from the Foothills Bull Bash Rodeo in South Dakota."

So rodeoing ran in Cruz's blood. She wanted to ask about his family but now wasn't the time. "I have breakfast on the table." She lifted Dani off the hood and set her on the ground. "Hurry and eat, then we can leave." Dani raced into the house. "You're welcome to join us or, if you'd rather, I can bring your meal out here." After their talk yesterday afternoon, Cruz had avoided the house and she'd left a supper plate for him inside the barn, where he'd worked until dark.

"I'm not hungry, thanks. I'll wait until you're ready. Take your time."

She wanted to point out that he'd probably need as much energy as possible if he was going to wrestle with a wild horse, but like her, he was a grown-up capable of making his own decisions. "Suit yourself." She returned to the house, made sure Dani finished her breakfast and then brushed her teeth and used the bathroom before they said their goodbyes to José.

"Call me when you arrive at the rodeo," he said, following them to the door.

Dani hugged him. "I love you, Papa."

It was almost comical to watch her father-in-law's face when Dani told him she loved him. The old man turned to mush when it came to his granddaughter. No matter how much he dug his heels in about moving, Sara seriously doubted he'd be able to watch Dani leave without him.

"I love you, too," he said.

Sara held the door open for Dani. "We'll be fine, José. Don't worry. Say hello to Betty and Leroy for me." She closed the door and didn't look back, but sensed José standing at the window watching the three of them get into Cruz's truck.

"When are we gonna be there?" Dani asked from the backseat.

Sara hid a smile behind a fake yawn.

"We haven't even left Papago Springs yet," Cruz said.

"I know." Dani stared out the window.

"What kind of music do you like?" Cruz asked Sara as he backed out of the driveway and drove off.

"Anything."

"Papa likes Johnny Cash," Dani said.

Cruz chuckled. "He does, does he?"

"Dani's grandmother was a big fan of Cash and after she passed away, José would listen to Sofia's CDs."

"Maybe I can find an oldies station." Cruz played with the radio until a Hank Williams song blasted through the speakers, then settled in for the long drive.

"Are we there yet?"

"Just about," Cruz answered Dani an hour and a half after leaving Papago Springs. He'd expected there to be tension between him and Sara after she'd learned he'd done time in prison, but he was surprised at how comfortable it felt to have her sitting next to him. He'd had a few girlfriends in high school, but he hadn't owned a car or taken a girl for a ride. One fateful night had robbed him of more than his freedom—it had stolen his youth.

He slowed the truck as he approached the Alamogordo city limits. The town's population boasted around thirty-five thousand residents but aside from the rodeo grounds there wasn't much to the place.

"Is this it?" The excitement in Dani's voice made Cruz smile. She reminded him of his brother, Emilio, who'd gotten excited about the littlest things—like their mother allowing them to dig through her purse for the change at the bottom, then walk to the drugstore to buy candy.

"I think the general parking is over there." Sara pointed out the windshield.

Cruz steered the truck in that direction and followed the line of vehicles entering the fairgrounds. While they waited to pay for parking, he removed his wallet from his back pocket and pulled out a ten-dollar bill.

"I'll pay for the parking," Sara said.

"You are paying." He gave her a small smile and her cheeks flushed a pretty pink. He liked that he could make her blush, but now that she knew he wasn't just a cowboy down on his luck but an ex-convict, it could be nervousness and not attraction that made her cheeks warm.

He paid the attendant, then veered across the lot and stopped behind the livestock barns. "I don't compete until noon," he said. "Once I sign in, we'll check the list of events. The smaller rodeos usually have activities for the kids earlier in the day before the main events."

"What kind of activities?" Sara asked.

"They might have mutton bustin' for the little ones or a pig catch."

"I've heard of mutton bustin', but what's a pig catch?"

"It's for older kids. They give them a burlap bag and

let a handful of small pigs loose in a pen. The kids have thirty seconds to try and catch a squealer."

"I don't like pigs," Dani said.

"Me, neither." Cruz set the parking brake and got out of the truck. While Sara helped Dani from the backseat, he removed his gear bag from the pickup and slung it over his shoulder, then put his hat on. Growing up in the city, he'd never thought he'd be the kind of guy who wore a cowboy hat, but when Riley Fitzgerald bought him a Stetson before he'd competed in a junior rodeo in Vegas a lifetime ago, Cruz had known the minute he'd set the hat on his head that he'd found his calling. He might have been born and raised in Albuquerque, but he was a cowboy of the Rio Grande.

"Nice hat," Sara said.

"Thanks." He nodded to the outdoor arena. "I check in over there."

They crossed the parking lot where a line of cowboys waited to register for their events. "You can stand in the shade if you want," Cruz said.

"We're fine. It's not too hot yet. When you're done, we'll buy a couple of water bottles and then I'll put sunscreen on Dani."

"I hate sunscreen. It's all sticky."

"I know, but you'll thank me later when you don't have wrinkles in your thirties."

"Name?" The man at the table spoke when Cruz stepped forward.

"Cruz Rivera. Saddle bronc."

The man looked up slowly and stared as if Cruz had grown two heads. He figured someone would have heard about him here at the rodeo—he just hoped they wouldn't make a big deal out of it.

"*The* Cruz Rivera?" the man asked.

He nodded. It was a hell of a thing for a man to be famous. Too bad his reputation in the sport had been carved out behind a razor-wire fence.

"Didn't hear that you got out," the man said.

Cruz was acutely aware that the people around him had stopped speaking. His skin burned and it wasn't from the sun's rays.

"I need my number."

"Yeah, sure." The rodeo helper handed him a number and two safety pins to attach it to the back of his shirt. "Your draw is Nobody's Business."

"What do you know about the bucker?" Cruz asked. He had no knowledge of the current roughstock champions.

"He bucks high and tight, then rolls to the inside. Doesn't do a whole lot more than that."

"Thanks." Cruz turned away but stopped when the man spoke.

"Heard you rode High Wire after he retired from the circuit."

High Wire was a four-time national champion and had been retired early for breeding purposes. The warden was close friends with the owners of the horse and that's how High Wire had shown up at the prison rodeo and it had been no coincidence that Cruz had been assigned to ride the horse. The owners and the warden had fully expected Cruz to get bucked off—no cowboy had ever ridden High Wire to the buzzer. Rumor had it that the warden and the owners had put money down on the ride, certain Cruz would get bucked off.

"Heard you made it to the buzzer, too."

"I did." Cruz grew uncomfortable with the attention and turned away.

"Good luck today!"

Breathing a sigh of relief, he stepped away from the table, glad that no insults had been exchanged in front of Sara and Dani. "Ready?"

Sara grabbed Dani's hand and they followed him through a maze of rodeo personnel, then stopped behind the livestock chutes. He set his bag inside an empty stall and handed a twenty to an old man sitting nearby. "I ride at twelve-thirty." The old man nodded as he took the bill.

When they walked off, Sara asked, "Why'd you give him money?"

"He watches the gear bags."

"He looked pretty old. Are you sure he won't fall asleep on the job?"

"He might." Cruz clutched Sara's elbow and guided her around a group of chatting buckle bunnies, then released his hold. "Most of the old men who hang around the rodeos competed in their day. A lot of them have injuries that prevent them from being able to work on ranches or do manual labor. So they show up at rodeos and offer to keep an eye on the cowboy gear for extra money."

"That's sad."

Sad, maybe, but a way of life for a lot of cowboys.

"I'm hungry," Dani said.

Sara sniffed the air. "I smell doughnuts."

"Let's check out the concession stand." Cruz allowed his nose to lead him. On the way they stopped at the event table near the main entrance and grabbed a flyer listing the day's events. Once they'd purchased a bag of doughnuts and water bottles, they sat at a table in the shade.

"The mutton-bustin' event is scheduled at ten-thirty. That's an hour from now," he said.

"Is Dani old enough?"

The sugar crystals at the corner of her mouth winked at Cruz and he tamped down the surge of desire that hit him when he thought of licking the sugar off her lips. "It's pretty safe. They make the kids wear a helmet and the sheep are tame."

"Would you like to ride a sheep, honey?" Sara asked.

Dani's cheeks puffed out as she chewed her doughnut. She nodded, then swallowed. "Can I win a prize?"

Cruz laughed.

"She's a little competitive." Sara laughed.

"I don't know if you win anything," Cruz said.

"I wanna ride." Dani finished a second doughnut, then wiped her mouth on a napkin and stood. "I'm ready."

"Let's see if there's still a spot open." They stood in another line and registered Dani for the event, then picked out a helmet that fit snugly on her head. "We'll sit over here and watch until they call your group." Cruz picked seats high in the stands so Dani could see into the chute, where the rodeo helpers put the kids on the backs of the sheep.

The chute doors opened and the first group came out—a little boy and two little girls fell off immediately. Dani glanced at Cruz. "They're not very good."

"It's harder than it looks," Cruz said.

"I bet I won't fall."

"It's not nice to brag, Dani," Sara said.

The next group of kids were placed on the sheep

and one of the animals walked out of his chute when the door opened.

"How come the sheep isn't running?" Dani asked.

"Some run. Others walk. You never can tell what the sheep might do," he said.

"I hope mine runs," Dani said.

"I hope yours walks," Sara said.

Cruz chuckled at the mother-daughter squabble, then his gaze met Sara's and for an instant it felt as though they were a family. Just as soon as the feeling came, it disappeared, leaving a hollow feeling in his chest.

Chapter Six

"You're ready," Sara said, tightening the strap of Dani's protective headgear. "But you don't have to ride if you've changed your mind."

"I wanna ride." Dani looked at Cruz, her brown eyes wide. "Will you put me on the sheep?"

"Sure thing." Cruz stepped forward and grasped Dani beneath the arms, then swung her over the back of the animal and held on until she found her seat.

The two could pass for father-daughter. Sara was at once sad for Dani that her daughter had lost her father early in life. And sad for Tony that his daughter had so easily entrusted herself to Cruz's care, as if she couldn't remember her father at all. Sara glanced at the sky—a habit she'd acquired after Tony had passed away. At first she'd wanted to believe he was looking down on them. Later, after the numbness of his death had passed, her glances heavenward were more like accusatory glares.

Hadn't Tony considered that eventually something bad could happen if he continued working at the clinic in the barrio? Why couldn't he have lived in the real world instead of a make-believe one, where he was every man's hero but no hero to his own wife and daughter?

"Take a picture for Papa." Dani preened.

Sara pulled her iPhone from her purse and snapped a few photos. Then she widened the image to include Cruz crouched next to Dani and clicked again. How could a man who was worried about a child injuring herself be a cold, hard criminal? Sara knew there had to be more to the story on how he'd landed in prison.

"Ladies and gents, we've got our final group of little wranglers ready to go in our mutton-bustin' competition this morning!" The announcer's voice boomed over the sound system and applause filled the outdoor arena.

"Up first is a pretty little filly named Dani. Can you wave to the crowd, cowgirl?"

Dani swung her arm back and forth—the child didn't have a shy bone in her body.

"Dani's riding on Eloise, a rough, tough bucker from the Madison ranch in Branch Springs."

"What if I fall, Mr. Cruz?" Dani asked.

"Then you hop up off the ground and run right back here," Cruz said. "But if you stay on until you hear the buzzer, you'll win a ribbon."

"Okay, I'm gonna win."

Cruz smiled, a true genuine grin that stole Sara's breath. Automatically she lifted the phone and snapped his image, then repeated the action when he swung his head toward her, his smile still in place. No man had a right to be that handsome.

"Go, Dani, go!" Sara shouted when the gate opened and a rodeo helper smacked the sheep's hindquarters. The animal trotted out of the enclosure and across the arena at an even pace. Dani's little body bounced up and down but she hung on, the crowd cheering encouragement.

The buzzer sounded. "Well, lookee there," the announcer bellowed. "Our little cowgirl got the best of Eloise. Congratulations, Dani!"

Cruz stepped into the arena and cupped his hands around his mouth, then shouted, "Slide off, Dani!" The sheep changed directions and trotted back toward the chute, Dani still clinging to its back. When it drew a few yards away, Cruz approached and lifted Dani off the sheep, then twirled her in a circle. The crowd applauded and Dani giggled.

"Now there's a great daddy-daughter picture!" Music followed the announcer's statement.

Sara's heart ached as she watched the pair. When Cruz headed down the road again, Dani would miss him. Had it been foolish of her to ask Cruz to stick around longer? Was she only making things worse for her daughter—never mind herself? She couldn't deny that she wanted something to happen between her and Cruz, even though a long-term relationship was out of the question. The acknowledgment made her admit that she'd be using him as her rebound guy after Tony's death and that seemed cold, especially when he treated Dani so well.

"Mama! Did you see me?"

Sara dropped to her knees and held out her arms. Dani's little body slammed into her and she squeezed her tight. "I sure did."

"I won!"

"Congratulations, honey." She glanced at Cruz and caught the unguarded look in his eyes as he watched her. The man was lonely and starving for affection. To lead him on would be cruel. "Are you hungry?" she asked her daughter, taking her hand.

Dani nodded.

"Let's find a concession stand and grab a snack." She walked off, assuming Cruz would follow. When he didn't, she stopped. "Aren't you coming?"

He shook his head. "I've got to get ready for my ride."

He wasn't competing for an hour. Maybe he wished to be left alone. "You can take Dani through the barns to see the animals," he said.

"Sure." She smiled. "Good luck with your ride." *And please, God, don't get hurt in front of Dani.* She walked away from the chutes, her feelings for Cruz in turmoil.

"He's nice, Mama."

Distracted by her thoughts, she mumbled, "Who?"

"Mr. Cruz."

"Yes, he is."

"I wish he was my daddy."

Startled, Sara didn't know what to say. Taking the easy way out, she pointed to the white barn across the parking lot. "Let's look at the horses before we grab a bite to eat." Maybe admiring the bucking stock would make her forget the lonely look in Cruz's eyes.

Now that Sara and Dani had walked off, Cruz took a deep breath. Damn his parole officer. Couldn't the man have waited another week before checking up on him? *You were living in a fantasy world. Someone had to knock some sense into you.*

He made his way through the throng of cowboys, gathered in groups entertaining each other with far-fetched rodeo tales. It was obvious that Sara felt uncomfortable around him now that she knew he'd done prison time. In all honesty he didn't know why she hadn't told him to pack his bags and leave.

An image of her pretty face flashed before his eyes. Maybe he did know why she hadn't kicked him to the curb. She was attracted to him. Why was anybody's guess. He had nothing to offer her.

Maybe she likes the idea of being with an ex-con.

He cursed himself for the uncharitable thought. Sara wasn't like that. She didn't use people. She was kind and gentle.

And lonely.

He might have been in prison for twelve years, locked away from the female race, but he wasn't so hard inside that he couldn't recognize emotion in another person. He had no idea what kind of relationship Sara had had with her husband, but there was no denying the aching need in her eyes when she watched him.

Cruz stopped in front of the old man who'd kept an eye on his bag. "Thanks." He reached for his gear but froze when the man spoke.

"I knew yer daddy way back when. He still in prison?"

Cruz nodded. His father had written several letters while Cruz had been serving his sentence but Cruz hadn't answered them. There was nothing left to say—he'd been a huge disappointment to his father, who'd expected better from his son.

"Heard it was self-defense."

"It was." When Riley Fitzgerald had flown Cruz to the South Dakota prison, his father had told him what had happened that night in the bar and it had been almost word-for-word the same facts Shorty had told

Cruz when they'd met at the Gateway Ranch, where Cruz had been sentenced by Judge Hamel to do community service after tagging an office building in downtown Albuquerque.

"Hell of a bull rider, your father. Ya ridin' bulls or broncs today?"

"Broncs."

The old man nodded to a group of cowboys staring at Cruz. "Don't let them wet-behind-the-ears goons get to ya."

"Why would they bother me?"

"Name's Roscoe, by the way." The geezer turned his head to spit tobacco juice on the ground. "They're all talkin' 'bout ya."

Let them talk. What did he care?

"They don't think yer as good as the rumors say."

"Just how good do the rumors say I am?" He was curious.

"Ya might be better 'n Ricky Sanez."

"Who's this Sanez guy?" Cruz had paid no attention to the sport while in prison. Some of the guys had kept up with the rodeo standings, but not Cruz—it was too painful.

"He's from Brazil. Don't speak a word of English but the kid can ride. They say he's gonna win the NFR this year."

Good for Ricky Sanez. Cruz wouldn't be riding in the big-money events. His shot at fame and glory had passed him by long ago. He was okay with that—or he thought, anyway. Today's ride would decide if he'd gotten rodeo out of his blood when he'd been in prison.

"I'm riding for fun," Cruz said. And because he owed a debt to Shorty.

"You'll be a regular on the circuit in no time."

Did the old man know something Cruz didn't? "I gotta go."

"Nobody's Business spins left coming out of the chute before he bucks."

The old man didn't have to tell him that—he was sure none of his competitors would have warned him. "Thanks."

"Good luck."

Cruz nodded, then moved into the shadows where he could catch his breath and let his guard down before he rode. He expected a few cowboys to know about his prison rodeo record, assuming the warden had bragged about Cruz's success to anyone and everyone who'd listen. But he couldn't let them get into his head.

He closed his eyes and conjured up an image of a bronc. He envisioned his ride even before he settled on the back of the bucker. In his mind's eye he went over every detail—his grip on the rope. His feet turned out, ready to mark the horse as soon as the chute opened. He pictured the bronc turning left, its neck tight against the inside of its body. He could feel the pressure of the spin, the force of the animal's momentum slamming into his chest. His muscles bunched and tightened as he struggled to keep his seat.

A deep chuckle interrupted his thought process and his eyes popped open. His gaze clashed with a cowboy a few inches taller and whose shoulders were a fair bit wider than Cruz's.

"Somethin' I can do for you?" Cruz said.

The man grinned. "Yeah, fall off Nobody's Business." A deep chuckle followed the statement. "In case you need a reminder, this ain't a two-bit prison rodeo. This is the big time."

Big time? He opened his mouth to correct the cowboy, but decided he'd let him believe he was a bigger deal than he really was. A commotion caught his attention and he spotted a reporter and cameraman heading his way.

"Looks like the jailbird's drawing a lot of attention. A shame how us law-abiding cowboys get the short end of the stick while you and your murdering dad get all the fanfare." The cowboy shot Cruz a glare, then walked off.

"You Cruz Rivera?" The reporter shoved a microphone in his face. "Mind stepping into the light and answering a few questions?"

"I do mind," Cruz said. When the reporter didn't back off, he swung his gear bag over his shoulder and shoved past the man.

The reporter followed him. "Is it true that you were a member of the Los Locos gang in Albuquerque?"

Cruz kept his gaze focused on the exit at the other end of the cowboy-ready area. He'd sit in a damned port-a-potty until it was his time to ride.

"And what about that inmate? Is it true you beat him up bad when he tried to get friendly with you?"

Only the slightest falter in his step hinted that the question got to Cruz. He hated that details of his life were being aired in public. He just wanted to be left alone—preferably ignored.

Before he reached the exit, Sara and Dani came around the corner. She took one look at his face and her smile vanished.

"Mr. Cruz!" Dani rushed forward, oblivious to the reporter and his cameraman. "We bought you a hot dog."

He took the hot dog from Dani's hand. "Thanks."

"Who's the lady and the kid?" the reporter shouted.

Cruz gave a hard shake of his head—a warning to Sara not to follow him. She grasped Dani's hand and stepped out of his path.

"Are you Cruz's girlfriend? Wife? Is that his daughter? What's your name, little girl?"

The questions were fired off in quick succession but Cruz kept walking, knowing it would be far worse for Sara and Dani if he remained by their side. He'd almost made his escape when one of the reporters said, "What's a pretty lady like you doing with a criminal? You got a thing for dangerous men? Aren't you afraid for your daughter?"

Cruz stopped dead in his tracks, then spun and returned to Sara's side in a flash, where he snatched the reporter by the shirt collar, then lifted the man up on tiptoes. "Leave the lady and her daughter alone. Understand?"

The reporter nodded. Cruz released his hold and the man stumbled until he regained his balance. He glanced sideways but Sara and Dani were already walking toward the stands. If he ever needed a reminder of why he had no business hanging around Papago Springs anymore, he'd gotten it this afternoon. As soon as they returned to José's, he'd pack his bags and head down the road. No amount of help repairing a barn was worth putting up with crude comments from reporters and who knew what else before the day was over.

"LADIES AND GENTLEMEN, it's time for the bronc-bustin' event!"

Sara smiled at Dani and clapped her hands, hoping to encourage her daughter to relax. After she'd witnessed Cruz grab the reporter by the scruff of his neck, Dani had grown quiet. Obviously she'd been affected by the chaotic scene they'd come upon a short while ago.

"This afternoon eight eager cowboys will try to prove they've got what it takes to ride the big buckers."

"What's a big bucker?" Dani asked.

Sara leaned close and whispered, "I overheard the man telling his wife next to me that the horses in this event are bigger and stronger than the ones we saw a few minutes ago."

"Oh."

Sara kissed her daughter's forehead. "Don't worry about Mr. Cruz. He'll be fine."

Dani's brown eyes widened. "Was Mr. Cruz gonna beat that man up?"

"No, honey."

"Why did he look so mean?"

"Because the man was being rude to us."

"I don't like that man for making Mr. Cruz mad."

"Me, neither." Sara pointed to the roughstock chutes. "Look. There's Mr. Cruz. See his white shirt?" Cruz's Western shirt stood out among the other cowboys, who wore bright colors with bold stripes.

"Is he gonna ride now?" Dani asked.

"Pretty soon." Cruz stood off by himself while his competitors gathered in a circle and exchanged laughter. She didn't know if it was because he wasn't a regular on the circuit or if it was because he'd been in prison, but for whatever reason, Cruz was ignored by the other cowboys.

"First up this afternoon is a newcomer to this rodeo. Cruz Rivera hails from Albuquerque by way of the White Sands Correctional Facility outside Las Cruces."

A quiet hush fell over the crowd and a lump formed in Sara's throat. Why had the announcer made that information public? Were they intentionally trying to get inside Cruz's head and affect his ride? A surge of anger shot through her and she balled her hands into fists, hating that there was nothing she could do to protect Cruz from their ridicule and prejudice.

"Some of you may have heard of the White Sands annual prison rodeo. Cruz Rivera is the all-time record holder in the saddle-bronc event. Let's see how this… cowboy handles a real bucker like Nobody's Business."

As if Cruz had ridden dummy horses in the prison rodeo.

Sara expected applause or at least a shout or two of encouragement, but the rodeo fans remained silent and the cowboys near the chutes stepped away, offering no help or encouragement as Cruz straddled Nobody's Business.

"What's Mr. Cruz doing?"

That Dani hadn't questioned her about the announcer's prison comments didn't surprise Sara. Dani was focused solely on Cruz. "He's tying the rope around his hand so he has something to hang on to." As soon as she'd spoken, Cruz nodded his head and the chute opened. The horse bolted and Sara's breath caught in her throat when she thought Cruz would fly backward off the horse. Then she realized he was leaning back on purpose and raising his legs high to spur the horse above the shoulders.

Time slowed to a crawl as Cruz and Nobody's Business appeared more like dance partners than adversaries. The fluid motion of his body as he rode through the horse's twists and bucks was a beautiful thing to watch. The cowboys who appeared uninterested only minutes before now clung to the rails, their gazes glued to the action.

Time ceased to exist and when the buzzer sounded, Dani jumped out of her seat. "Did he win?" she shouted.

The fans around them stared as Sara coaxed Dani to sit down. "We have to wait and see what the judges think."

Cruz leapt off the bucking bronc and amazingly landed on his feet. His hat had flown off after the first buck and he walked a few feet away and scooped it from the ground, then headed to the open chute.

"Well," the announcer said. "Looks like Cruz Rivera took care of business on Nobody's Business."

The crowd remained silent.

"Let's see what the judges think."

A minute later the scorers' table lit up with a seventy-nine.

Sara knew enough about rodeo to understand that was not a winning score. Maybe Cruz had made a mistake during his ride and the judges had marked him down for that.

"Looks like our first score of the event is beatable. Next up is a young rookie from Santa Fe. Let's give Mark Hall a warm welcome."

The crowd applauded and clapped and that made Sara angrier.

"C'mon." She stood. "We'll find Mr. Cruz and congratulate him on a great ride." She took Dani's hand and they made their way out of the stands. They hadn't even arrived at the cowboy-ready area before Cruz intercepted them.

"Let's go," he said, his face a blank mask.

"I saw you ride, Mr. Cruz!" Dani's voice was filled with excitement.

Cruz's heart squeezed painfully. The kid had no idea how much he needed her smile right now. But the worried look in Sara's eyes reminded him that they had to get out of there before...

"Hey, jailbird!"

Cruz stiffened but didn't acknowledge the voice behind him.

"Where are you running off to? Don't you want to stick around and watch a real cowboy bust a bronc?"

"Keep walking," Cruz said, his eyes on the exit. He'd gained plenty of experience ignoring taunts from fellow inmates but he had his limits, and if he was pushed too far, he'd fight back. He didn't want to get into an argument in front of Sara and Dani. It was humiliating enough that they heard the taunts.

"You run away, Rivera! We'll meet up again and I'll beat your sorry ass in the arena!"

As soon as they stepped outside, Cruz grasped Sara's arm and practically pulled her to his truck across the parking lot. Dani had to run to keep up with them. By the time they got into the vehicle and backed out of the spot, a crowd of cowboys had gathered near the entrance to the arena—a cowboy send-off party. Lucky him.

Was this what waited for him at every rodeo he entered? Had Shorty even considered that Cruz might be ostracized by his rodeo family? When he reached the town limits, the silence inside the truck was as thick as glue. *Damn it*. This was supposed to be a fun day for Sara and Dani.

"Are you all right?" Sara whispered.

Her question sounded like nails on a chalkboard and he winced. He glanced in the rearview mirror. Dani stared out the window with a forlorn look on her face. When his eyes returned to the road, he spotted a root-beer stand and said, "Anyone hungry for ice cream?"

"I am!" Dani shouted.

He swung the truck into the parking lot. "I haven't had a root-beer float in a long time." He hopped out, then helped Dani from the backseat. Maybe if he pretended nothing out of the ordinary had happened this afternoon, Sara would play along.

Fat chance.

"Dani," Sara said, "why don't you see what kinds of ice cream they sell." Dani raced over to the adobe café and stared at the pictures of treats on the board nailed to the side of the building.

Cruz forced himself to meet Sara's gaze. "I don't want to talk about it." If she believed he'd offer an explanation for today's events, she was mistaken.

"I don't understand why they treated you the way they did."

Was she really that naive, or was she just trying to get him to open up and share his feelings? Typical female—always wanting to chat about their feelings. Well, he didn't have any feelings left after his stint in prison.

Then what was that sensation you felt when Dani looked at you back in the arena?

Okay, he'd admit that prison life hadn't stripped him of all emotion, but he'd really have to be a hard-ass to not feel anything when a child looked at him with hurt and confusion.

"I'm concerned that—"

"Don't."

Her eyes widened. "Don't what?"

"Don't act like you care that I was ridiculed."

"But I do care. Is that going to happen at every rodeo you enter?"

"I doubt it," he lied.

"I don't think you should compete anymore."

He chuckled—better to laugh than slam his fist into the truck door. Busted knuckles would take care of entering another rodeo. But then he'd let Shorty down and he'd already let too many people down in his life.

"I hardly think this is funny," she said.

"I'm leaving Papago Springs in the morning."

"You promised to stay and repair the barn."

"That was before."

"Before what?"

"Before someone asked if you had a thing for ex-cons."

Chapter Seven

The drive home to Papago Springs took forever and the one source of chatter Sara had counted on to help the time pass quickly was sleeping in the backseat. She cast a sideways glance at Cruz. His face was an expressionless mask, but his white-knuckled grip on the steering wheel sent a silent message that he was livid. Embarrassed. Maybe even a little hurt, although he'd never own up to those feelings.

"You're really good," she said. "You make bronc busting look easy."

His stiff shoulders relaxed a little. "I had a lot of practice in prison."

"I wasn't aware prisons had rodeos."

"Most of them don't. White Sands has been doing it for a while." Thankfully Cruz kept the conversation going. "Before I landed there, I competed in a junior rodeo competition in Las Vegas. I'd never planned to follow in my father's footsteps, but that day I discovered that I liked the challenge of trying to best a wild horse. I was hooked after that ride."

"How many rodeos did you compete in before..."

"Only a few. But I placed in the top three each time."

He released a harsh breath. "Then life happened and my plans for a rodeo career went down the drain."

"It's nice that you had the opportunity to compete in prison."

The knuckles whitened again. "Each year that I was in prison I liked rodeo less and less." He blew out a harsh breath. "Riding in an arena with razor-wire fencing wasn't what I had in mind when I was younger."

"You made the best of it." Trying to put a positive twist on a bad situation wasn't an easy task.

"I didn't have a choice. I was told I was competing whether I wanted to or not. I decided that if I had to ride I was going to win."

Sara nibbled her lip, then threw caution to the wind. "You earned a better score than a seventy-nine, didn't you?"

"I'm not a judge, but my ride was darn near perfect." He glanced her way and the emptiness in his brown eyes hurt to look at. "But I expected a low score. They wouldn't allow an ex-con to win."

"If they're going to cheat you, why bother competing?"

"I promised someone I'd ride the circuit until I figured out a plan for the future."

It wasn't any of her business but she yearned to know if she and Dani played a role in his future. "Have you decided where you'll go from here?"

"Not yet."

She ignored the weird feeling that skittered up her spine. Silence followed his comment and she thought for sure he was done talking, then he said, "I was offered a job at a boys' ranch outside of Albuquerque."

"Boys' ranch?"

"My high school teacher married a rodeo cowboy with money. He bought a ranch and they named it after her deceased brother. The Juan Alvarez Ranch for Boys. It's a place for at-risk teens."

"How do they determine who gets in?" she asked.

"A judge decides. When I was seventeen I got caught tagging a business, but instead of sending me to juvenile detention, the judge let me work off my community service hours at a local ranch. That's where I learned about rodeo."

"Will you take the job at the boys' ranch?" The couple who ran the ranch must believe, like her, that Cruz was a good man at heart.

"I don't know."

Sara wished he'd accept the job. They might not have a future together, but she'd like to know where Cruz ended up and that he was okay.

"I don't get it," he said.

"What's that?"

"Doesn't it bother you that I'm an ex-con? Don't I make you nervous?"

She laughed and he fought a smile. "You being an ex-con doesn't make me nervous." *You being a sexy, virile man does.*

"I make José nervous. He doesn't like having me around."

Sara waved a hand in front of her face, then checked over the seat, making sure Dani still slept. "You don't make him nervous. You remind him that Tony is dead." *And he sees that I'm attracted to you and doesn't think you're good enough for me.* "And all the work you're doing is making the move to Albuquerque more real for him."

"He must get lonely living by himself."

"He won't admit to it, but he is lonely and I feel guilty for putting pressure on him to move in with us."

"Why do you feel guilty? Seems like you're the one who will be sacrificing if he lives with you."

"Not really. I need José to help watch Dani when I'm at work. I could put Dani in an extended day-care program, but it's expensive and I don't want to use Tony's life insurance policy to pay the bills. I'd hoped to save the money for Dani's college tuition."

Cruz took the freeway exit to Papago Springs. He admired Sara's strength and doubted there were many women who would choose working longer hours over cashing an insurance policy to make ends meet. And the saddest part was that Tony's death was senseless. Then again he'd learned the hard way that a lot of things in life made no sense.

Cruz thought back to the days he'd run wild with his homies and the pranks they'd pulled. If he hadn't gotten caught tagging a building he would surely have joined the Los Locos gang, and the night Sara's husband died he might have been there. Hell, it might have been a bullet from his gun that had killed him.

"Cruz?" Her eyes darted everywhere in the cab but at him. "Will you tell me what happened?"

She wanted to know how he'd landed in jail. He hated talking about that day—would just as soon forget it had ever happened. He'd let too many good people down. He should have said no when Vic had asked him to go with him to confront Salvador Castro. But Cruz and Vic had been friends since they'd walked to kindergarten together—there was no question whether he'd go. He hadn't been a fool to accompany Vic; he'd been a fool to believe nothing would happen. Something bad always happened when you were dealing with gang members.

"It was an accident," he said. "My friend's sister got knocked up by a gang leader and the guy refused to take responsibility for his kid. Vic thought he could convince the guy to marry his sister. I didn't know he was carrying a gun." Cruz slowed the truck, the memory sucking him back in time.

"Castro laughed in Vic's face and insulted his sister, insisting he could have her anytime he wanted and there was nothing Vic could do to stop him. That set Vic off and he pulled a gun from the waistband of his jeans. I didn't think. I just grabbed the gun, shouting at Vic not to shoot. He struggled with me but I got the gun away from him. Then someone kicked my feet out from under me and I fell backward. When I fell to the floor, the gun went off and the bullet hit Castro in the shoulder."

"What happened next?"

"I figured one of Castro's homies would shoot me dead on the spot, but everyone ran except Castro, Vic and me. We were there when the police arrived a minute later. The next thing I knew I was sitting in the back of a patrol car, handcuffed, and Castro was on his way to the hospital."

"Didn't Vic set things straight?"

"He tried. He talked to the police for hours, insisting the gun was his and he'd been the one who shot Castro. There were too many witnesses. The police booked me on manslaughter charges."

"A good lawyer would have straightened that out," she said.

"Riley Fitzgerald, my high school teacher's husband, offered to pay for a lawyer, but I refused his help."

"Why?"

To this day, Cruz wasn't sure why—at least that's what he wanted to believe. But deep down inside him—so deep he'd gone there only once, because he almost hadn't made it back out—he'd believed it was his destiny. Like father, like son—he was headed for jail. He'd tried to do right. He'd earned his GED. But in the end even the help of well-meaning people couldn't exorcise the barrio out of him and he was exactly where he'd been meant to be since the day he was born.

"Why did the judge sentence you to twelve years? That seems excessive for an accidental shooting."

"I got four years."

Sara gasped. "What happened to extend your sentence?"

It wasn't pretty. Wasn't something he wanted to share with Sara. But he needed to set her straight—make her understand why she shouldn't be attracted to him.

"Before my parole hearing, I'd competed in four prison rodeos and each year they grew more popular. The warden made big money off ticket sales."

"He didn't want you to leave, did he?"

Sara was a smart lady. "The warden was worried ticket sales would drop and jeopardize his reputation."

"What did he do?"

"He sent a thug known for raping prisoners to change my mind about leaving."

Sara's eyes grew wide and her mouth opened but no words came out.

"I fought back and hurt the guy pretty bad. They

added eight years to my sentence. I refused to rodeo, but after getting jumped too many times to count I decided I'd rather ride broncs than get beat up anymore."

"And eight years later, when you came up for your parole hearing, what happened?"

"I threatened to go to the press with my story if the warden tried to keep me there. It worked." Cruz pulled into Papago Springs and parked in front of the cantina.

"It seems so unfair," she whispered.

"Your husband's death wasn't fair, either."

She nodded, her eyes shiny with unshed tears.

Don't cry for me, Sara.

"Are we home?" Dani sat up and rubbed her eyes.

"Go tell Papa you're hungry." Sara helped Dani from the backseat.

"I'm not hungry," Dani said.

"Go see Papa. He missed you."

Dani raced inside, leaving Cruz alone with Sara. They stared at each other over the hood of the truck. She was the first person he'd told about the attempted rape and he felt as if he stood naked before her eyes.

"I'll finish covering the hole on the side of the barn, then I'll pack my bags and leave."

"Stay."

He wanted to. More than anything. "I've stayed too long as it is."

She moved around the hood and stopped in front of him. "Stay until all the repairs are done."

Sara was asking too much of him. After today he felt raw inside. Maybe even a little desperate. He didn't trust himself to keep his hands off her. "No."

"Please." She inched closer and her feminine scent hypnotized him. "I don't want you to go."

"If I stay…" He couldn't make himself say the words.

"I know." Her eyes softened. "Let's take it one day at a time."

He'd been forced to take it one day at a time in prison and that's the last thing he wanted to do with Sara. She wasn't a one-day-at-a-time woman and the thought of using her—because that's what it would be when there was no future for them—bothered him more than it should for a man who was just freed from the slammer. But strip away the prison uniform, the gang tattoo, and he was just a man. A man who yearned to be with a woman who would make him feel good inside. And worthy.

"I'm not asking for anything more from you. I just…" She dropped her gaze for a moment, then looked him in the eye. "I just need you here." Her voice cracked and he nearly lost the battle to stand firm.

"I can't stay." He stepped by her and headed for the barn. He didn't know whether he was a fool or a coward. The one thing he knew for sure was that he was no saint.

"How was your visit with Leroy and Betty?" Sara joined her father-in-law at the kitchen table.

"Leroy's becoming forgetful. Betty had to finish half his stories for him."

"How old is Leroy?"

"Seventy-nine."

"You live to be seventy-nine and you're entitled to forget a few details." She'd noticed José's memory wasn't as sharp as it had been a few years ago. She'd heard that a traumatic event in a person's life could affect their memory and losing his wife and son had been a tough blow.

"Is Betty still volunteering for Meals on Wheels?"

"Two days a week. She's trying to talk Leroy into taking a cruise."

"That sounds nice. How are their grandchildren?"

José scowled. "If you want to know everything about them, you should have stayed here and ate supper with us."

Obviously José didn't care to talk about his friends, but Sara wasn't up to an interrogation about today's trip to the rodeo, either.

"Dani said no one clapped for Cruz after his ride." José sipped his coffee. As was their nightly routine, she helped Dani with her bath and José read her a story before turning out the light, then they sat at the kitchen table and talked about their plans for the next day.

"The crowd wasn't very accepting of him," she said.

"Did he step out of line with anyone?"

"No. Cruz isn't like that, José. He minded his own business and kept to himself." She sighed. "But then a reporter hounded him and his competitors taunted him and—"

"Did he expect others to welcome an ex-con with open arms?"

Her father-in-law had a difficult time accepting Cruz because of his past, but José didn't know him the way she did—he hadn't seen the wounded look in Cruz's eyes this afternoon when he hadn't known she was watching him. "Cruz wasn't looking for attention."

"He should have thought of that before he shot a man."

"He told me about that night," she said. José's eyebrows rose into his hairline but he remained silent.

"It was his friend who had pointed the gun at another man and Cruz tried to intervene. When he wrestled the gun away it went off by accident and he shot the man in the shoulder."

"If it was an accident, then why was Cruz arrested?"

She shrugged, not wanting to give her father-in-law too many details. This was Cruz's story to tell, not hers, and she doubted he'd want her talking on his behalf.

They sat in silence, Sara's gaze flickering to the kitchen door, where the sound of hammering echoed in the air. "He's leaving soon."

"Is he finished with the barn?"

"No." Sara's eyes stung and she blinked rapidly. Good grief, she hadn't cried or gotten emotional over anything in a good long while. She couldn't afford to break down. Someone had had to be the strong one after Tony died and José had sunk into depression.

"You don't want him to go."

Sara couldn't look her father-in-law in the eyes. "I was hoping he'd finish fixing up this place so we could find a buyer or renter." She shoved her chair back. "It's been a long day. I'm going to bed." Halfway down the hall she heard the screen door creak as José left the house.

CRUZ SENSED HE was being watched as he pounded the hell out of two-by-fours. The hammering had been a therapeutic end to a stressful day and he wasn't ready to stop bashing wood. He sucked in a deep breath through his nose but didn't catch the faint scent of Sara's perfume. Dani had gone to bed a while ago. That meant either a stranger had wandered onto the property or José had something on his mind.

He set the hammer aside and waited for his visitor to speak.

"Sara said you rode well today."

Cruz wasn't fooled. José didn't care about his ride. He cared about what his daughter-in-law and granddaughter had been subjected to at the rodeo. "I competed in the prison rodeo and made a name for myself." Unfortunately that reputation had followed him outside of prison.

He faced José. "I should have won today." He wasn't bragging. He was stating a fact. Then he dropped his gaze and studied the toe of his boot. "Rodeo fans are loyal and supportive. They don't want to see an outsider with a prison record come into their arenas and beat the local sons."

"Are you going to continue to compete?" José asked.

"I have to." *For Shorty.* And because he didn't know what the hell else to do.

"I don't want Sara or Dani going along you with again."

If Cruz were in José's shoes, he wouldn't want his loved ones trailing after an ex-con and being subjected to humiliating ridicule. "That won't be a problem. I'm leaving tomorrow."

"You haven't finished all the repairs."

Cruz narrowed his eyes. "I'd think you'd be happy that I was walking off the job, because you don't want to sell or rent this place."

"You're right. I don't want to leave. But leaving will make Sara and Dani happy."

"And me leaving should make you happy." He forced a halfhearted smile. "Looks like everyone's happy now."

The old man's scowl grew dark. "I want better for my daughter-in-law than you."

Cruz raised his hands in the air. "Hold on, now. There's nothing going on between me and Sara."

"I know, but she sees something worthy in you that I don't." José wasn't giving his permission for Cruz and Sara to explore a relationship, but he sure wasn't putting up any roadblocks. He turned away and left.

What the heck? Alone again, Cruz tossed the hammer aside. He stretched out on the hay bale and stared at the ceiling, noticing places that needed to be patched.

José had given Cruz permission to stay. Sara wanted him to stay. Dani liked him. Despite his history, this family was willing to give him a chance. Would it hurt to spend a few more days here? Make good on his word and finish the barn so Sara, Dani and José could move on with their lives? He didn't want to leave Sara in a jam but if he remained on the property, it would be tough not to let his guard down with her.

"Cruz? Are you in here?"

Sara. He held his breath, hoping she'd leave.

"There you are." She moved closer to the bales, stopping in the shadows, where he couldn't read her expression. "I came out to see if you were hungry. I could make eggs and toast."

"No, thanks."

"Thirsty?"

He sat up and rested his arms on his thighs. "José was just out here."

"Oh, really?" Sara pretended to be surprised but

Cruz could tell she knew darn well her father-in-law had paid him a visit.

"He doesn't care if I stay on a little longer."

"I'm glad." She wrung her hands in front of her. "We need you."

"I'm the last person you need hanging around this place, Sara." He stood and, because he couldn't resist, he touched her—tucking a strand of hair behind her ear. He let his finger caress the soft patch of skin on the back of her neck and he swore he felt her shiver before he pulled his hand away.

When was the last time he'd touched something so soft and feminine and had actually taken the time to appreciate it? *Never.*

He stared into her blue eyes. How could a nurse, a widow and the mother of a five-year-old appear so innocent and trusting? Or maybe any woman would have appeared innocent in his eyes after all the evil he'd seen and lived through in prison.

He sensed something special about Sara. He knew he'd never come across another woman like her after he left Papago Springs. With that thought in mind he lowered his head slowly, giving her the opportunity to rebuff him. She didn't.

Somewhere in the back of his mind, as he pressed his lips to hers, was the thought that this was almost like a first kiss. He couldn't remember the last girl he'd kissed or had wanted to kiss. Sara would be his new memory—one he feared wouldn't fade with time no matter who he met down the road.

Her breath feathered across his face as he swept his mouth over hers. He wanted to be gentle, but years of

dreaming of women tested his patience and he deepened the kiss.

She didn't resist. She pressed herself against him
and the feel of her soft breasts sent a jolt of electric-
ity through his body. He set his hands on her waist—
whether to pull her closer or push her away, he didn't
know. His fingers clamped down hard on her hip bones
when she wound her arms around his neck and thrust
her tongue inside his mouth.

The kiss grew hotter, wilder and sweeter. And Cruz
soaked it all in—the sweet taste of her, the soft feel of
her and the sexy smell of her. When she pulled back,
he wasn't ready for the kiss to end. He used all his
strength to release his hold on her.

"Please stay."

As if he had a choice anymore? "I'll stay under one
condition."

"Which is?"

As much as it killed him to say it, he knew he had
to. "No more kisses."

She spun toward the barn doors.

"Sara," he called after her.

"What?"

"I mean it."

Her smile tugged a groan from him. After she left,
he sucked in a deep breath, then exhaled slowly. It
hadn't taken much for her to sway him to stay. He felt
safe in Papago Springs and even though it was only
hours from the prison, it felt like a million miles.

When he'd first arrived, he'd wanted to be left alone
to do his work, but Dani's sweet personality, Sara's
kindness and even José's quiet presence had begun
filling the hole inside him—an emptiness he'd thought

he was immune to but wasn't. Sara's sunny smile and Dani's laughter made him feel as if he were home and that surprised the heck out of him, because not even his mother had made his childhood house feel like a home. His real home had been wherever he'd hung out with his homies—street corners, abandoned buildings and salvage yards.

Papago Springs felt like home.

As long as he remembered the fairy tale had to end. Nothing good lasted forever.

Chapter Eight

"Looks like you landed in a good place." Riley Fitzgerald offered Cruz his hand.

Surprised by his former mentor's appearance, Cruz was momentarily speechless.

"I'm Dani. Who are you?"

"Hello, Miss Dani." Fitzgerald tipped his hat to the little girl. "I'm Mr. Fitzgerald. I'm friends with Mr. Rivera."

Dani squinted up at Cruz. "Who's Mr. Rivera?"

"Me," Cruz said.

"Oh." Dani inched closer to Cruz and Fitzgerald quirked an eyebrow.

"Dani is José's granddaughter."

"My mom's name is Sara," Dani said.

Cruz looked at Dani. "Why don't you go inside and see if your mother needs help."

"But I was helping you," she said.

"We're almost done here."

She stuck out her lower lip, then spun and marched to the house.

"Spirited little thing," Fitzgerald said.

"She's a good kid."

"What's the story with these people?"

"Dani's father passed away a while ago and Sara's been trying to convince her father-in-law to move to Albuquerque and live with them."

Fitzgerald glanced around. "Looks like you're fixing up the place."

"Sara hopes to sell or rent the barn and land before they return to the city."

"Are you getting paid?"

Cruz nodded. "How did you find me?" Not that he'd intentionally tried to hide from people.

"You created quite a stir this past weekend in Alamogordo."

The rodeo gossips were probably having a field day.

"I heard you made it to eight and then some on Nobody's Business."

"The judges didn't think my ride warranted more than a seventy-nine."

Fitzgerald shook his head. "You planning to compete again?"

"The letter from Shorty…" Cruz swallowed hard. It was tough to believe the old man wasn't here anymore.

"He died of a heart attack in his sleep."

"At the Gateway Ranch?" Cruz asked.

"Yep. He had no family, so Maria had his body brought to our ranch and we buried him there."

"He'd like that." It occurred to Cruz that he ought to ask about his mentor's wife. "How's Maria?"

"Busy with the twins."

Cruz had forgotten that his former teacher and her husband had twin sons. "How old are the boys now?"

"Clint and Wes turned seven this past May."

Cruz smiled. "I bet they're a handful."

"They are." Fitzgerald took off his hat and twirled

it on his finger. "I tracked you down for a couple of reasons. First, I thought you might be ready to take on a full-time job, but it appears you've already put roots down."

"There's nothing going on between me and Sara. As soon as I repair the barn, I'm heading out." And Sara, Dani and José would leave for Albuquerque.

"I also stopped in because Victor contacted me and asked how you were. I assumed you'd have spoken with him by now."

Cruz still struggled with his feelings toward his former best friend and didn't know how to answer Fitzgerald, so he asked, "What's Vic up to?"

Fitzgerald pulled a folded piece of paper from his pocket and handed it to Cruz. "That's his number. Call him and find out."

He shoved the note into his pocket, sure it would stay there for a long while.

"If this doesn't work out—" Fitzgerald waved his hand "—you've got a job waiting for you at the ranch."

Cruz already knew *this* wasn't going to work out.

"Maria would love to see you again."

He figured his teacher was the real reason behind Fitzgerald's visit. Maria Alvarez Fitzgerald had saved Cruz from joining a gang only to lose him to prison anyway. She'd done so much for him and he'd let her down. Right now he didn't have the courage to look her in the eye. "I'll keep the job in mind."

Fitzgerald set his hat on his head. "Cruz?"

"Yeah."

"Don't disappoint Maria."

The words struck Cruz like a fist across the chin, and he swayed.

"I won't. You have my word."

"Good." Fitzgerald pulled out a wad of hundred-dollar bills from his pocket. "Take this. You never know when you might need a little extra cash."

There had to be at least a thousand dollars in rolled-up bills. Yeah, the money would come in handy but Fitzgerald had already done enough for him. "Thanks, but I'm good."

"Maria doesn't want you sleeping on the streets."

"I'm not." He motioned to the trailer. "I've got a bed."

Fitzgerald frowned. "Suit yourself."

Cruz followed Fitzgerald to his truck, then shook his hand. "I appreciate everything you and Maria have done for me."

"Wouldn't have it any other way. You're family." Riley shut the door and drove off.

Family. He guessed Maria viewed him as a younger brother. But as much as he wanted to embrace the idea…he'd rather be a part of the family living inside the house thirty feet away.

"WHO'S THAT MAN talking to Cruz, Dani?" Sara asked when her daughter walked into the kitchen.

"Mr. Fitz… I can't remember. He's Mr. Cruz's friend."

So this was the wealthy man who'd helped Cruz years ago. "Did he say what he wants?"

Dani shrugged.

"Stop interrogating the child." José frowned.

"Why don't you wash up for supper." After Dani left the room, she said, "I believe his name is Riley

Fitzgerald. He once helped Cruz and his friends when they were having trouble in high school."

"There's plenty of food. Invite him to supper."

"Good idea." Sara hurried into her bedroom to brush her hair and powder her nose. By the time she left the house, the taillights of the visitor's truck were a spec on the horizon.

Cruz stood in the driveway, watching his friend leave.

"I'd planned to invite him to join us for dinner," she said, announcing her presence.

"He had business to take care of."

Why did Sara sense Cruz didn't want her to meet his friend? "Was that Riley Fitzgerald—the man who introduced you to rodeo?"

"He was a hell of a saddle-bronc rider." The admiration in Cruz's voice rang clear and loud.

"He stopped by to see how I was doing." Cruz swung his gaze to Sara. "And to find out if I'd changed my mind about working for him."

"Where did you say his ranch was?"

"About an hour north of Albuquerque. Why?"

Sara spotted a suspicious gleam in his eye. Had he guessed what she was thinking—that an hour outside of Albuquerque wasn't that far from where she lived? That if he took the job maybe they could see each other after José got settled in with her and Dani?

Cruz was the first to look away. Then his chest expanded and he released a harsh breath. "The barn roof is fixed."

Already? Only a week had passed since they'd returned from the rodeo. Then again he'd put in fourteen-hour days—eventually the job would get done. Sara

wasn't ready for him to leave. Selfishly she wanted him
to stay until it was time for her and Dani and José to head
north. And her father-in-law would never admit it, but
Cruz's presence at the ranch was pulling him out of his
depression. Witnessing the improvements to the property
had put a spring in José's step. Maybe she was jumping
to conclusions, but there might be a small chance that
Cruz was filling the void left by Tony's death.

"I was thinking that we should fence the property.
Divide it up into sections so horses could be separated
if several owners were boarding at once." Dollar signs
rang up in her head and she knew she should feel some
guilt that she'd have to use Tony's life insurance to pay
for the materials, but she was desperate to keep Cruz
in Papago Springs a little longer.

Their gazes clashed, his filled with turmoil. She
understood she was making things more difficult between them but nothing with a man like Cruz would
be easy. "If the property was fenced, we could charge
more for boarding."

"Is José okay with your plans?" he asked.

"I haven't asked him, but I'm sure he'll see it makes
sense."

"It's going to cost money for all that fencing." His
gaze pierced her as if he wanted to make sure she knew
that fence posts weren't the only cost she'd have to deal
with if he stayed.

"I know," she said, answering the obvious question—and the unspoken one.

Seconds ticked off the clock before he ran his fingers through his sweaty hair. "If José wants the corrals, I'll stay. If he doesn't…"

You'll leave.

THE CITY OF Deming Cowboy Park was crammed with pickups and horse trailers as cowboys arrived for the annual rodeo. Cruz parked in the back of the dirt lot, near the exit. He wanted to cut out early—as soon as he finished his ride—then hightail it back to Papago Springs and Sara.

The trailer on José's property was beginning to feel like home. Or maybe it was the people, not the place, that felt like a comfortable fit. He couldn't remember the last time he'd ever been content, at peace. Being around Sara had a calming effect on him. It didn't matter that he was attracted to her and dreamed of making love to her when he went to bed every night—her presence soothed his battered soul and he swore as the days went by that he noticed a different feeling growing inside him.

Slowly, a little bit at a time, the emptiness in his chest was giving way to a feeling of hope. The pent-up anger he'd carried for so long seemed like a lifetime ago. It took more effort to remember that his best friend had dragged him into a fight that hadn't been any of his business. Or that his father had abandoned his family. That his mother hadn't reined in Cruz when he'd started running with a gang. Each time Sara smiled, more and more resentment drained from his body.

He grabbed his gear and headed to the sign-in table. The rodeo was PRCA–sanctioned and he expected there to be talented cowboys competing this afternoon. A tingle of excitement raced through his blood and this time he didn't try to tamp it down. He wanted to compete—not just to honor Shorty's memory, but because he wanted to win. It was a different feeling than he'd had in prison, where he'd been expected to win. Prison had stripped away his love of the sport—until he'd slid onto the back of Nobody's Business and felt the urge to show off. Today was all about proving himself. And he didn't care if his competition called it beginner's luck.

He made his way to the cowboy-ready area. He rode in two hours, but he'd arrived early to watch the other events. The trick would be avoiding reporters once they spotted his name on the saddle-bronc roster. He slipped into the shadows behind the chutes and watched the team-roping event. A half hour passed before a group of young contenders stopped nearby and began talking.

"Don't worry, Sean. Victor Vicario's riding on nothing but luck. He's bound to lose one eventually. Maybe today's the day."

Victor Vicario? Cruz's mind raced back to his conversation with Fitzgerald. The man hadn't mentioned that Vic had taken up rodeo. Since when had his friend wanted to bust broncs? The last Cruz knew, Vic had decided getting bucked off a horse wasn't his idea of fun. Vic hadn't been interested in rodeo in high school. He'd wanted to make a fast dollar—legally or illegally—didn't matter.

Cruz wondered how long Vic had been riding. Maybe if he'd followed the rodeo circuit like the other convicts in prison, he might have come across Vic's name in the standings. A surge of jealousy ripped through his gut. Vic was living the life Cruz had planned for himself until fate had intervened. Fitzgerald had given him a taste of what a rodeo career would be like and Cruz had embraced the thrill and the challenge wholeheartedly. He'd known in his heart and by the looks on the faces of the rodeo judges that he had the talent to be a top contender one day.

He'd set a goal for himself, determined to rise above his father's tarnished reputation, the gangs, his weak mother and a bad home life. Deep in his gut Cruz knew if he'd stayed out of prison he'd have beaten the odds and won a national title by now. But instead of him basking in success, it was Vic who was living the life Cruz had wanted. Cruz had had to settle for riding in prison rodeos on has-been broncs. His moment of glory came one day a year, then he went back to being inmate 1376 until the next rodeo.

"There he is," a cowboy said, then a hush fell over the group.

Cruz stepped farther into the shadows. He couldn't get a good look at Vic because his cowboy hat was tipped low over his face. His friend had filled out over the years and turned his baby fat into muscle.

"He's nothing but a has-been gangbanger. He's a loser. You got nothing to fear from him."

Cruz squeezed his hands into fists as anger filled him. After all these years the urge to come to his friend's defense was still there. He'd leave him to handle his own battles—things hadn't turned out so well the last time he'd tried to save Vic from himself.

"He was lucky last week in Amarillo."

"He's lucky every week." A cowboy with red hair adjusted his Stetson and swaggered toward Vic. Cruz couldn't hear the exchange between him and Vic. When carrottop returned to his friends, he said, "The man's full of crap."

"What did he say?"

"He said I should go change out of my diapers because toddlers aren't allowed to compete today."

Cruz swallowed a chuckle. That sounded like something Vic would say. He'd always enjoyed taunting others—probably because he'd been taunted about the scar on his face growing up.

The group moved off, giving Cruz a clear view of Vic. He stood alone—like Cruz. They were both outcasts. He wished things hadn't ended the way they had between them or he might have caved in and walked over to say "Hey," "Good luck," "How've you been the past twelve years?" Now wasn't the right time. Shoot, Cruz didn't know if there would ever be a right time.

The announcers warmed up the crowd as he waited for the saddle-bronc event to begin. He kept an eye on Vic—still standing alone. A trio of buckle bunnies approached him and flirted but as far as he could tell, Vic wasn't interested, his face a mask of concentration as he studied the horse in the chute next to him.

"Ladies and gentlemen, we're kicking off the saddle-bronc event next and we've got a stellar lineup of cowboys this afternoon, not to mention a great group of broncs."

As Cruz listened to the announcer run down the list of competitors, his ears perked when Vic was mentioned.

"Victor Vicario has been moving up the ranks the past few years and it looks like he might have a shot at going to Vegas this December if he can keep his seat through Cowboy Christmas."

Vegas? Vic was that good?

"Vicario hails from Albuquerque and he's coming out on Jumpin' Jack. That's right, folks, you heard me… Jumpin' Jack. This bronc can jump clean out of the chute if he wants to."

Vic climbed the rails and straddled the bronc. It was like looking in the mirror—the way Vic wrapped the roped twice around his hand only to unwind it, then repeat the process all over again. Cruz's mind flashed back in time to when Riley Fitzgerald had taught them how to hold the rein and Cruz had rebelled, claiming his way was better. Riley had finally conceded that Cruz's way worked for him and had quit pestering him to change his grip. He'd had no idea that Vic had paid attention to Cruz and now used the same routine when he rode. Cruz wasn't sure how he felt about that— maybe a little pissed off and a little honored.

Next, Vic sank low in the saddle, pushing his hips forward and his shoulders back. Cruz usually leaned a fraction to the right—his strong side. Vic did the same thing and sat slightly off balance. Then he reached for the brim of his hat and pulled it low, hiding half his face—just like Cruz. Out of instinct he counted to five, then nodded.

Jumpin' Jack sprang into action, kicking straight out before snapping back and hitting the ground. Vic stayed on, his backside rising off the saddle before coming down hard. Cruz couldn't help but be impressed with the way Vic held his arm high above his head as the bronc kept up its relentless spinning.

Glued to the action, Cruz didn't realize he held his breath until he heard the buzzer, then a gust of air shot from his lungs. "Look for an opening, Vic. There it is." Cruz spotted it a second before Vic flung himself sideways and hit the ground shoulder-first. He sprang to his feet, grabbed his hat and ran for the rails. He didn't wave his hat at the crowd before he disappeared behind the chutes.

Cruz was impressed. Vic was a natural at the sport. Why hadn't his friend told him he'd taken up rodeo? Hell, Vic could have written him a note while Cruz had been in prison. And never once in any of the birthday or holiday cards he'd received from Maria had she mentioned Vic's rodeo career. It was as if everyone had purposefully kept it a secret.

You know why, don't you?

Because Vic had robbed Cruz of the chance to pursue a rodeo career. They all probably thought Cruz would be miffed or wish Vic ill will. He hoped he wouldn't have felt that way, but who knew. Those first few years in prison had been rough and he'd hated just about everyone in the world—and Vic had been at the top of his list.

He couldn't change the past. Couldn't wipe out his prison experience. Couldn't magically claim what should have been his—a rodeo career. Maybe what hurt the most was that he no longer wanted the rodeo career he'd once dreamed of having. Yeah, he still felt the thrill before a ride, but the all-consuming desire to make it to the top had fallen by the wayside in prison. He kept his eye on Vic, who collected his equipment. No one stopped to congratulate him. If he'd been riding the circuit for years he should have made a few friends, but from where Cruz stood, Vic appeared all alone.

"Ladies and gents, get ready for the second ride of the afternoon!" The announcer's voice echoed through the stands, ending Cruz's mental contemplation. "This cowboy also hails from Albuquerque and he's going to take on a bronc named Sassy Sally."

Cruz tugged on his riding glove and walked over to the chute a few feet away.

"Although he didn't win in Alamogordo last weekend, rumor has it this cowboy put on quite a show. Let's see if Cruz Rivera can top Vic Vicario's ride."

Cruz climbed the rails and settled onto Sally's back. The bronc stood steady while he wrapped the rope around his hand. He lifted his head one last time and his gaze connected with Vic's. Other than the pasty color of his friend's face, Vic showed no emotion.

Cruz tugged his hat low then sucked in a deep breath and nodded. Come hell or high water, he was going to show Vic he was the better saddle-bronc rider. He nodded and the gate opened.

Sally didn't spin—she twisted when she bucked. She turned her head and chest to the left but her back end swung right, which tormented Cruz's spine. As if the ride happened in slow motion, he blocked everything from his mind but the bronc. The noise in the arena faded to only horse grunts and hooves thudding against the dirt.

He and Sally danced for what felt like minutes, not seconds. When the buzzer sounded, Cruz kept his arm in the air—more out of habit after showing off for the prison crowds than because he wanted to prove he was just as good as Vic. Sally's bucks grew weaker. The crowd noise faded. Everything came to a standstill, including the horse.

Among a silent crowd, Cruz jumped off Sally, patted her rump, then scooped his hat off the ground. Head high, he walked out of the arena and went straight for his gear bag, avoiding eye contact with everyone.

"Rodeoing in prison ain't the same as being in a real rodeo, convict!"

Here we go again.

"We don't want you here. So stay the hell off the circuit. We got women and children traveling with us. We don't trust you around them."

Cruz bit his tongue.

"You'll give rodeo a bad name."

Right then the announcer called out his score. "Looks like Cruz Rivera will have to keep practicing, folks. He scored a seventy-six on his ride. Vic Vicario is still the cowboy to beat."

"You're not one of us, Rivera. Go home and stay home."

"Back off, Davis."

Cruz recognized Vic's voice—a little deeper than high school but the same tone.

"Why are you coming to his defense?" The cowboy gaped at Vic. "He's an ex-con."

Cruz tensed when Vic stopped in front of his tormentor. "He's a rodeo cowboy first. The rest doesn't matter."

Cruz thought that was a little naive but nice of Vic to believe that.

"Stay away from rodeo, jailbird. You're tarnishing the sport." Davis swung his fist, landing a blow to Cruz's jaw. The pain reverberated through his skull and he stumbled backward.

"You stupid ass," Vic said, stepping between the men.

"I don't know why you're defending a piece of shit, Vicario, but if he doesn't stay away from rodeo,

I won't be the only one throwing punches at him."
Davis walked off.

Cruz threw his bag over his shoulder. He had to get out of there before he or Vic got into a brawl. He made a move to leave, but Vic grabbed his arm.

"Wait."

"I've been doing nothing but waiting the past twelve years. I'm done waiting." He jerked his arm free.

Vic winced, the action stretching the scar from the corner of his eye, across his cheek and through the edge of his mouth. The puckered flesh was a reminder of Vic's rough childhood.

Vic visibly struggled to speak and Cruz took pity on him. "Nice ride today." He turned away and left the arena.

Chapter Nine

It was midnight and Cruz still hadn't returned from the rodeo. Sara stood in the backyard, staring at the dark trailer. She'd gone to bed at ten-thirty but had tossed and turned until she'd finally given up and stepped outside for fresh air.

The day had passed quietly without Cruz's presence—no hammering or sawing sounds coming from the barn. Just a stillness that reminded her she was alone. Not physically alone—she had Dani and José with her—but emotionally *alone*. After grieving for Tony, Sara had given herself permission to move on. She hadn't been looking to date or get involved with any men, but she'd decided if one happened along, she'd be open to the possibility of a new relationship.

She never thought she'd test the waters with a man like Cruz Rivera. In some ways, she felt guilty for wanting a deeper connection with Cruz but not a long-term relationship. She'd already experienced being with a man who focused only on himself and his goals. She'd be a fool to believe that after getting out of prison Cruz would be ready to put the needs of others first. It would only be natural for him to focus on himself. To go where he wanted to after being behind bars for twelve years. She didn't want to put limits on that freedom. He deserved to pursue his own goals and dreams and she refused to stand in his way.

But she was lonely and yearned for intimacy. The passion and attraction she'd once felt for Tony had faded a tiny bit each night he'd come home from the clinic and regaled her with stories of people he'd helped rather than listen to her tell him about her or Dani's day. On the rare occasion when they made love, it was just sex—a quick fix before Tony ran out the door in the morning.

The sound of a truck engine pulling into town caught her attention. She released a deep breath, grateful Cruz had returned. She hadn't been worried that he'd take off and leave for good—not after spending the morning cleaning the trailer and doing his laundry. And snooping. Yes, she admitted she hoped to find something in his personal possessions that would tell her a little more about him. But there had been nothing. No books. No letters from home. Not even a watch or a ring. It made her sad that he possessed so little—everyone should have something they treasured.

A crunching sound met her ears before Cruz's shadow cleared the edge of the house. He stopped walking when he noticed her. There was just enough light from the moon to make out his dark figure. Only the occasional chirp of a cricket broke the silence.

Heart pounding, Sara moved closer. "How did you do?"

"I lost."

She smiled at his disgruntled tone. "There's always next time." She secretly rejoiced in his loss. He'd have to stick around longer and earn more money to pay the next entry fee.

"You're up late. Everything okay?"

"Fine. I dusted the trailer today and put your clean clothes on the couch."

"You didn't have to wash my clothes."

"I wanted to." She inched closer.

He stared into the darkness and balled his hands into fists.

"Did something happen at the rodeo?"

He opened his mouth, then snapped it closed and shook his head.

She touched his arm and the muscle beneath hardened like a rock. "Tell me."

He shrugged free and walked to the trailer, disappearing inside without a word. No way was she going to let him off the hook that easy. When she entered the trailer, Cruz stood at the sink with his back to the door. She remained silent, waiting for him to acknowledge her.

"I ran into an old friend." He faced her.

She pointed to the purple bruise along his jaw. "Did your old friend do that to you?"

Cruz's lips curved—he was so handsome when he allowed himself to smile. "I didn't get into a fight. I got punched."

Her nursing instincts kicked in and she went to him. Gently she pressed her fingers along the bone, watching his reaction as she increased the pressure. "I don't think it's broken or fractured." She rubbed her knuckles against his day-old whiskers, enjoying the scratchy feel. "You should put ice on it."

She forced herself to look into his eyes and his stare

made her shiver. She dropped her arm and reached for his hands. There wasn't a scratch on them. Cruz hadn't fought back, because fighting would violate his probation. He'd rather get beat up than risk going back to jail. Her heart broke for him.

"I'm sorry."

"For what?" He threaded his fingers through hers.

"For stupid people doing stupid things," she said. That he didn't pull away caused her blood to pump hard and fast through her body. "Tell me what happened." Did he trust her enough to open up to her?

"Same thing as last weekend." He stared at his boots. "They don't want an ex-con in their midst."

Sara heard a world of hurt in that simple sentence and she wished she could take away his pain. Make him forget the humiliation. She rocked forward on her toes and kissed the bruise along his jaw. He stiffened. Then she moved her mouth along his cheek, pressing tiny healing kisses to his skin. He smelled like leather and faded cologne. When she reached his ear and sighed, he grasped her arms.

"I can't," he said.

She stared into his eyes. She'd have to be a moron not to recognize the heat and hunger in his gaze. "Why not?"

"You deserve better." He left her standing in the kitchen and retreated to the bedroom, shutting the door behind him.

Frustrated and a little miffed that Cruz had rejected her, Sara left the trailer and returned to the house. A half hour had passed when she heard footsteps in the hallway followed by the bathroom door opening and closing. The shower turned on and the pipes rattled in the wall behind her bed.

She closed her eyes and envisioned Cruz naked beneath the spray of cool water. Envisioned soap suds rolling down his chest, his thighs, the bubbles pooling at his feet before being sucked into the drain. Caught up in her fantasy, she didn't notice that the water had shut off. The glowing digits on the nightstand clock flipped to a new minute. Then another. And another.

Mind made up, she left her bed and rummaged through the sock drawer in her dresser. When she found the coin purse she'd hidden away, she removed three condoms from inside. After Tony had been gone a year, she'd purchased the protection *just in case*. She had intended to be prepared if the time ever came when she had sex again.

Condoms clutched in her hand, she stepped into the hallway. The bathroom door stood open. Cruz had left the house already. She slipped her feet into her flip-flops and walked out to the trailer. Cruz stood in the living room with a bath towel tied around his waist.

She jutted her chin. "I'm a grown woman and I think I know what I want and what's good for me."

Anger flared in his eyes for two seconds before it died away. She cut through the kitchen and stopped in front of him. "I'm not asking for promises. Just tonight."

He closed his eyes when she pressed her palm against his naked chest and dragged her fingernails over his smooth flesh, stopping to pluck his nipple before playing with the knot at the front of the towel.

If she undid the knot, there would be no turning back and Cruz wasn't going to be the one to make that decision for her. She tugged on the terry cloth and the towel fell to the floor. As she studied his naked body, an old familiar ache that she hadn't felt in a long time sputtered and came to life inside her, warming her blood.

He cupped her jaw, tilting her head up. He stared into her eyes, then his lashes fluttered closed and he pressed his mouth to hers. She'd braced herself for a hungry, all-consuming kiss, but Cruz surprised her with his gentleness.

Small nibbles, tiny bites and slow, lingering brushes of his tongue threatened to melt her. He pulled her against him, his hardness pressing into her stomach. His hands caught the edge of her pajama top and he whisked it over her head, then dropped the material on the floor. A guttural groan reverberated through him when their naked chests bumped together. He buried his face against the side of her neck and held her close. Time stood still.

Cruz inhaled Sara's sweet scent, the softness of her naked breasts caressing his chest, making him light-headed. He'd dreamed of holding a woman in his arms since he'd gone to prison, but he hadn't imagined she'd be as special as Sara. He tucked her closer, as if he could absorb her into his body and make them one.

Then fear took over. Not the fear that he wouldn't or couldn't be gentle. Fear of what happened when it was all over—when Sara tossed back the bed covers and left the trailer. Once he tasted Sara, he worried he'd never get his fill. How could he walk away from her and move ahead with his life if he carried this memory with him?

Sara nuzzled his neck. "Take me to bed, Cruz."

He didn't have to be asked twice. He didn't understand why she was giving him the gift of herself, but until she'd touched him he'd had no idea how badly he needed that human connection. He didn't know what he'd done to deserve this night with Sara, but he counted his blessings and swept her up into his arms and carried her to the bedroom. He set her on the bed and, with her help, tugged off her clothes. Gently he lay on top of her, balancing his weight on his elbows. He wanted to tell her that he cared about her. That this meant a lot to him. That he needed her as he'd never needed a woman before, but the words would be meaningless coming from an ex-con.

Her smile shot an arrow through his heart. "Make love to me, Cruz."

Make love. "I've never made love before. It was always just sex."

Her blue eyes turned misty. "Then I'll show you how to make love." She reached for his hand and placed it over her breast.

That was all the encouragement he needed and for the first time since he'd left prison, he lowered his guard and allowed himself to simply *feel*. Not so much in the physical sense. He opened himself up to an emotional connection with Sara, consequences be damned. Fate had brought them together just like fate had made him wrestle the gun from Vic's hand. This time he was more than glad to allow fate to take its course.

A QUIET SNORING sound drifted into Sara's ears, but her eyes remained closed as she concentrated on the rise and fall of the chest beneath her cheek. Her hand rested over Cruz's heart, which thudded slow and steady. A kaleidoscope of memories flashed through her mind as she replayed their lovemaking. He'd been gentle—almost too careful, forcing her to coax him to let go.

The experience had been more than she'd bargained for. More than she'd ever dreamed and it saddened her that she and Tony had never shared such intimacy as her and Cruz had. Maybe if they had, their relationship would have been better.

If only she'd met Cruz before Tony—maybe both their lives would have taken different paths. *Then you wouldn't have Dani.* Sara smiled as her daughter's precious face flashed before her eyes. Dani was her world now. It was up to Sara to raise her—to be both a father and a mother to her daughter. Maybe someday a man would happen along who'd make a great father for Dani.

But tonight had been about her—just her. Tomorrow would come soon enough and her time with Cruz would be a memory she'd cherish for the rest of her life.

"Regrets?" he whispered into the dark.

Sara stretched across his body and found his mouth. After thoroughly kissing him she said, "None."

"Good." He flipped their positions and propped himself up, then spent the next five minutes exploring the sensitive areas of her body, teasing her until she squirmed and begged for mercy, which he granted her a long time later. When Sara woke next the sky was a light purple. The sun would rise soon and she needed to return to the house before Dani or José woke.

Carefully she extricated herself from Cruz's arms and left the bed. Then she gathered her clothes off the floor and made her way to the door, pausing a moment to watch him sleep. He looked innocent with his eyes closed and his mouth partially open. She wished with all her heart he hadn't had to go to jail for trying to help a friend. And she wished with all her heart that gangbangers hadn't shot her husband and taken his life.

Why did good people have bad things happen to them?

She wouldn't learn the answer to that question staring at Cruz. She left the bedroom and closed the door. After slipping into her pajamas, she found her flip-flops and returned to the house. She'd almost made it to her bedroom when José's door opened. His knowing gaze rattled her. Unable to find her voice she went into her bedroom. José's footsteps echoed down the hall as he walked to the kitchen.

She couldn't hide in her room all day and she couldn't go back to sleep if she tried. She might as well have it out with José before Dani woke. After changing clothes she looked in the mirror and cringed. Her mouth was swollen from Cruz's kisses. There would be no denying what they'd done.

Steeling herself for a confrontation, she went into the kitchen. José sat at the table staring into a cup of coffee. When he didn't look at her, she removed a mug from the cupboard, poured herself a healthy dose of Folgers and sat across from him.

"It just sort of happened."

Her comment brought his head up. "Nothing sort of happens with you, Sara." He shifted his gaze to the wall behind her. "I remember when Antonio brought you here for the first time. I knew then that you were the levelheaded one in the relationship. Antonio, God rest his soul, was a dreamer."

That was true. Tony had had plans and dreams of

starting up a mobile health clinic in the barrio. He wasn't sure where he'd find funding for it, but the logistics hadn't mattered. He'd assumed others would figure that out when the time came.

"You think I don't know what kind of husband Antonio was?" José stared Sara in the eye.

"What do you mean?"

"He confessed to me that he didn't spend enough time with you and Dani, but he couldn't stop himself from working."

Jealous that Tony had confided in his father, Sara held her tongue.

"Antonio left you and Dani alone a lot, but—" he nodded to the back door "—Rivera is not the right man for you. You can do better."

"Better how?"

José narrowed his eyes. "What do you know about his family?"

She dropped her gaze.

"You can tell a lot about a person by his relationship with his family."

She resisted the urge to ask if his relationship with Tony was the reason Tony had put himself before his loved ones, but didn't because José meant well and only wanted to protect her and Dani from getting hurt. "Cruz doesn't talk about his family."

"You need to ask him. He just got out of prison. Why didn't he go home to see his mother? What about his father? Does he have brothers and sisters?"

If she told José what Cruz had shared with her about his father it would only upset him, but she resented José for putting a damper on what she and Cruz had just shared. Although his concerns were valid, she'd rather live in a fantasy world and pretend Cruz had no past.

"A man like Cruz has enemies. Being with him could put you and Dani in danger."

Sara hadn't considered that someone from Cruz's past—a person who wanted to do him harm—might use her or Dani to get back at him. She gulped her coffee. She'd been selfish and foolish to encourage Cruz to stick around. She'd condemned her deceased husband for only thinking about himself and she'd committed the same sin, putting her needs and desire to be with Cruz before what was best for Dani.

"I'm hungry." Dani stood in the kitchen doorway rubbing her eyes.

José patted his knee and Sara's daughter climbed into his lap and snuggled against his chest. "Mr. Cruz said he's gonna fix the flat tires on the bike he found in the barn."

"What bike?" Sara asked.

"The blue bike." Dani straightened and clasped her grandfather's cheeks with her tiny hands. "Papa, Mr. Cruz said you could teach me how to ride."

"I could," José said.

"I wanted Mr. Cruz to teach me but he said grandpas were better teachers."

Sara set a mug of water in the microwave to heat for Dani's oatmeal. There was no denying her daughter was growing close to Cruz and she guessed José's criticism of the man might have a bit to do with jealousy.

"Mama?"

"What?"

"I like Cruz 'cause he talks to me when I'm bored."

Sara kept busy making the oatmeal so she wouldn't have to see the knowing look in her father-in-law's eyes.

"My daddy never talked to me."

"Your daddy was a busy man, honey."

"How come?"

"Remember he was a doctor and he helped people?"

"How come my daddy didn't never help me?"

José set Dani in the chair next to him, then left the table. A few seconds later Sara heard his bedroom door open and close. For everyone's sake she should tell Cruz to move on and then hire someone else to finish the repairs on the barn. But after making love with Cruz, feeling his loneliness…knowing that she'd filled a void in him—even if it was temporarily—letting go was more difficult.

Tony had never held her in his arms the way Cruz had—with an urgency that bordered on desperation. A heady feeling for a woman who'd always felt as if she were an afterthought.

Sara set the bowl of oatmeal in front of Dani. "Your daddy did help you, but you were too little to remember."

"Oh."

"Hurry up and eat," Sara said, refilling her cup of coffee. She stopped in front of the kitchen window and stared at the trailer. Was Cruz still sleeping or had he snuck off to the barn when she hadn't been looking?

She was hungry for another glimpse of him, recalling the way his hands had stroked her body. Warm tingles spread through her and she breathed deeply, almost believing she smelled his masculine scent in the kitchen.

"There's a man at the door, Mama."

Sara stepped away from the sink and discovered they had a visitor. That the man had come to the back door surprised her. "I'm sorry," she said, "the restaurant isn't open on Sundays."

"I'm looking for Cruz Rivera."

What did he want with Cruz?

"My name is Ed Kline." He reached into his shirt pocket and removed a business card. "I'm Cruz's parole officer. He said he was doing handyman work in Papago Springs and his truck is parked out front of the restaurant."

"Cruz has been making repairs to my father-in-law's barn. He's staying in the trailer across the yard."

"Thank you, ma'am." Ed Kline made a beeline for the trailer. Sara watched but Cruz didn't come to the trailer door. The parole officer headed for the barn and disappeared inside.

"Mama?"

"What, honey?"

"What's a parole officer?"

"I don't know," she lied. "I think he's a friend of Mr. Cruz." Whatever his reason for coming here today, it wasn't a social call.

"You didn't check in with me last week."

Cruz spun and came face-to-face with his parole officer. The shorter man was stocky with a thick neck—probably a wrestler in high school or college. "I've been busy."

Kline moved closer and stared at Cruz's face. "So the rumors are true?"

"What rumors?"

"You got into a fight at the rodeo in Deming yesterday?"

"I didn't get into a fight. I got hit."

"Same difference."

"Not really. I didn't defend myself. I walked away."

Kline's gaze bore into Cruz as if he were judging for himself whether or not Cruz was lying. "I brought some forms you need to fill out." He motioned to Cruz's face. "If you plan to keep being used as a punching bag you might want to sign up for the government health care program I mentioned."

"Is there another reason you drove all this way to find me?"

Kline nodded. "Seems you've got some friends in high places."

Cruz had no idea what the man was talking about.

"Judge Hamel called our department after you were paroled. She spoke to a few people on your behalf and you've got a couple of job offers sitting on my desk." He gestured to the barn. "There's no need for you to work for room and board."

Cruz suspected Judge Hamel had contacted Gil Parker, the owner of Gateway Ranch, where Shorty had been employed and Cruz had worked off his community service hours. He wasn't ready to be around people yet. He liked that it was just him fixing José's barn. "I'll think about it once I finish this job."

Kline shook his head. "I don't normally track down parolees. If they don't respond to my calls I turn their name in to the police and let the officers find them."

"Why are you here, then?"

"Because you're so darn special, Rivera, that's why." He snorted. "The judge and a few others in higher places don't want anything to happen to you. As a matter of fact, you're a bit of a celebrity after all the rodeo records you set in prison."

Celebrity. Hell, he'd trade his star power any day for a normal life and anonymity.

"You can't go around to rodeos getting beat up. If you're going to keep competing you have to stay out of trouble."

"What do you know about rodeo?"

"I was a bull dogger in my day. Rodeo cowboys are a tight bunch and they especially don't want someone like you out-shining them in the arena."

"Then they should learn to ride better."

Kline nodded. "I agree, but the fact is no judge is going to score you high enough to make any money. Not an ex-con. Staying on the circuit will land you back in prison, because one of these days you will hit back and get arrested."

"I can't stop. Not yet. Made a promise to a friend that I'd stick it out until I was ready to settle down somewhere."

"Then you'd better settle down soon. If anything happens to you, my head will be in the meat grinder."

"Don't worry. I'm sticking to the smaller rodeos. I won't be going back to any PRCA-sanctioned events." He didn't care to meet up with Vic again. The idea that his friend was living the life Cruz had planned for himself made him angry and sad. He was better off avoiding Vic.

"Here." Kline handed Cruz a phone card. "There's five hours of talk time on the card. Use it. I want to know what rodeos you're riding in and I want to know when you leave Papago Springs." Kline walked to the barn entrance. "And you'd better fill out that damned paperwork and mail it in. I don't want Judge Hamel breathing down my neck if you get hurt at a rodeo and can't pay for a doctor."

"Aren't you going to search the trailer and my pickup?"

"Nope. You know why?"

Cruz remained silent.

"Because you're too smart to screw up again."

Chapter Ten

"I'm ready."

Guilty of being caught staring out the window when she should be cleaning tables, Sara flashed a hesitant smile at her father-in-law.

"Looks like Cruz is off to the dump again," she said. Since Monday he'd taken several loads of junk from the barn to the landfill. All that was left to do was order clean hay for the horse stalls and hook up the new water hoses—then the barn would be ready to rent out.

"You didn't hear me," José said.

"I'm sorry. What did you say?"

"I'm ready to move back to Albuquerque with you and Dani."

For a moment Sara didn't know what to say, then she found her voice. "That's great. Once we find a renter—"

"We don't need to find a renter before we leave."

"I don't understand."

"The sooner we go, the better."

She dropped her gaze, pretending to wipe at a stubborn stain on the table in front of her. "Is this sudden change of heart because of…" Five days had passed since José had discovered she'd slept with Cruz, and things between them had been cordial but strained.

"The restaurant is losing money."

The business had been running in the red for several years.

"Better to cut my losses."

She had a difficult time believing him after he'd dug his heels in for years. Even Tony had tried to convince his father to retire after Sofia had passed away, but he'd refused.

"I'm not getting any younger and Dani will be grown up before we know it. I want to spend time with her."

Sara wished that for her daughter, too. "Then we have a lot of packing to do. I'll contact the Realtor and tell him to get started on the paperwork to list the property."

José left the room and Sara sat down and willed her thudding heart to calm. This was what she'd wanted all along after Tony died. So why did it feel wrong?

Because you have to say goodbye to Cruz.

They hadn't spoken more than a few words to each other since Sunday but that hadn't bothered her. They'd both needed time to adjust to what had happened between them. But she hadn't thought they'd be parting ways afterward. She'd believed they'd have until the end of July—another month to be together. Then, when her leave of absence from the clinic ended, she'd return to Albuquerque.

No sense agonizing over José's decision. Maybe it was best to end things with Cruz sooner than later, even though the yearning to make love with him again was almost too powerful to ignore. She tossed the cleaning rag aside and went into her bedroom. She might as well make a detailed list of things that needed to be done. First things first. She'd contact the Realtor and get the property listed.

WHEN CRUZ RETURNED from the dump, he found Sara waiting for him in the driveway. And she wasn't smiling. He'd done his best not to be caught alone with her since he'd made the mistake of making love to her. Sara had kept her word and had shown Cruz how tender and intimate making love with a woman could be. He hadn't thought himself capable of tender touches, whispered words or deep, long gazes into a woman's eyes, but Sara had shown him that prison hadn't stripped him of everything—he was still able to show emotion. Feel emotion. Which made it all the more difficult not to pull her into his arms and whisk her off somewhere private.

His gut clenched at her troubled expression. Had José guessed that Cruz had crossed the line with his daughter-in-law? He wouldn't doubt it. The older man had barely said a word to him all week.

He parked the truck and got out. He hated the thought that Sara might have to pay penance for the few hours they'd spent together.

He stopped in front of her and studied her worried expression. All he'd thought about the past few days was the burning need to kiss her. Hold her. Caress her silky hair and trail his fingers over her naked hips. He hungered to hold her close and breathe in her scent.

When he recalled their lovemaking, it was the snuggling that he'd enjoyed most. The sex had been hot and untamed but afterward, when they were lying in each other's arms, Cruz had felt most at peace.

"Everything okay?" he asked.

"I have something to tell you."

"What is it?"

"José has agreed to move to Albuquerque."

That was good news, wasn't it?

"He wants to leave Saturday morning."

"This coming Saturday?"

She nodded.

Damn. The fantasy world he'd been living in was coming to an abrupt end. Ignoring the pang in his chest, he said, "What can I do to help?"

"I called the Realtor and he's listing the place tomorrow." She gestured toward the house. "José's packing the canned and boxed foods. The rest he's giving to Charlie. I phoned Jill to let her know José was moving and wouldn't be here to check on her father."

How was Sara going to fit everything in her SUV and José's truck? Maybe he should follow them and take some of their things in his pickup. As soon as the thought entered his mind, he nixed it. He'd violate his probation if he returned to Albuquerque without his parole officer's permission. Kline had asked Cruz to keep away from the city the first six months after his release so he wouldn't become involved with a gang. Not that he would be tempted.

As much as he wanted to support Sara, he couldn't risk word getting back to Kline that he'd been to Albuquerque. No way was he returning to prison for a parole violation. Once he was behind bars the warden would make sure Cruz stayed there a good long while.

"I've rented a small trailer and I'm driving into Las Cruces tomorrow to have the dealership install a hitch on the back of my car."

"Have you ever towed a trailer before?"

"No, but it's not that big. I'm sure I'll be fine."

She didn't have to convince him. Beneath all her soft beauty was a layer of steel. He couldn't believe he hadn't asked her this before. "Would your parents or maybe a sibling help you make the drive?"

"I'm an only child. My mother and stepfather live in France. I only see them every few years."

No wonder it was important to Sara to keep close with José. The man was all the family she and Dani had left. He wished he could help her with the move.

"We'll be fine." Her shoulders straightened. "I talked it over with José and he said you're welcome to live in the trailer as long as you want or until the place sells."

Staying in Papago Springs was out of the question— too many memories. Saturday morning he'd hit the road and ride the circuit full-time.

"Is there a chance you might take that job working at your friend's ranch?" The spark of hope brightening her blue eyes made his chest ache.

"Maybe one day I'll end up there." Working for Fitzgerald and living an hour from Sara would be pure torture. "What needs to be done before Saturday?"

"I called TLC Ranch. They're delivering a load of hay for the horse stalls tomorrow. I'll need that stowed in the barn."

"Anything else?"

"We could use your help loading the furniture in the morning."

"You got it." He nodded to his truck. "I promised Dani that I'd take her for ice cream this weekend. Maybe I could take her now, since you're leaving Saturday."

"Sure."

That she trusted him to be alone with her daughter and believed he'd never let anything happen to Dani humbled him.

If she knew you'd associated with the gang who killed her daughter's father, I doubt she'd be as trusting.

"I'll tell Dani you're waiting out here."

"You're welcome to come along." To hell with his plan to keep his distance from Sara. They had less than forty-eight hours together.

"I need to keep packing." She fled inside the house.

As soon as the door shut behind her, he kicked a rock across the road. He'd been fooling himself these past few weeks—living in a bubble with Sara, Dani and José. Pretending he wasn't the man he really was.

The door opened and Dani dashed across the driveway. "Mama said you're gonna take me to get ice cream."

Cruz chuckled at her excitement, then his laughter faded when he realized he'd not only miss Sara, but Dani, too. The thought of not knowing what would become of this little girl who'd lost her father to gang violence bothered Cruz. He wanted to know that she'd be okay. That nothing bad would happen to her—ever.

It was sobering to realize that if he'd never gone to prison he'd never have met Sara, Dani or José. Until now, he'd believed prison had taken away what he'd wanted most—a rodeo career. But fate worked in mysterious ways and maybe there was a reason he'd gone along with Vic to confront the gangbanger that fateful night. Maybe prison had saved his life.

But it had also stolen his dreams.

Dreams can change.

Dani tugged on his jeans. "What's the matter, Mr. Cruz? You look sad."

He crouched in front of the child. "I'm not sad, Dani. What flavor of ice cream do you want?"

"Vanilla with sprinkles on top."

"A confetti cone." He walked over to the truck and opened the door for her. "Hop in." At least Dani would take his mind off the inevitable for a short while. Because no matter how hard he wished it not to be true, he and Sara were parting in less than forty-eight hours.

"What's your favorite ice cream?" Dani asked as Cruz drove out of town.

"I like vanilla, too." The simple, sweet flavor reminded him of Sara—wholesome goodness.

"Are you gonna come to Albuquerque with us?" she asked.

"No."

"Are you gonna stay at Papa's?"

"I don't think so." The nearest Dairy Queen was twenty-three miles away. Dani had time to ask a hundred questions before they arrived.

"Why not?"

"I have more rodeos to ride in."

"I like the horses, but rodeos stink." She pinched her nose.

Cruz rubbed his hand over the ache throbbing in his chest. He'd never considered himself father material—never given a thought to being a father one day. But his protective feelings toward Dani had him contemplating the subject. Even though he was an ex-con, could he still be a good father? He'd grown up without a father figure during his teen years, and he wondered if he'd had a male role model in his life back then if he'd still have run with a tough crowd. T.C. Rivera had been one of the top bull riders in the country when he'd gone to prison. If he hadn't gotten into the bar fight after the rodeo that night in South Dakota, he would have been around to teach Cruz to rodeo. Who knew—maybe Cruz would have won a national championship before his thirtieth birthday.

He glanced in the rearview mirror. Who would watch over Dani when she entered her teen years and boys showed interest in her? Would Sara be married by then, or single? Would José be alive to make sure the boys treated Dani with respect? When he thought back to his teen years and how he'd treated girls… He'd been a slave to his hormones and had never once considered that the girls he'd coaxed into having sex with him were somebody's daughters. "Dani?"

"What?"

"Boys are yucky, right?"

"My friend Charity says boys have cooties."

"Charity's right. Don't let a boy get close to you."

"Tanner tries to pull my pigtails."

"You tell Tanner if he doesn't stop, I'll make him." Dani's eyes widened. "What are you gonna do?"

"I'll hang him up by his socks on the monkey bars." Dani giggled. "Mr. Cruz?"

"Yeah?"

"I wish you could come to Albuquerque with us."

"Me, too, Dani. Me, too."

SARA CLOSED THE back door quietly and made her way to the barn. José had gone to bed over an hour ago, exhausted from packing and making decisions about what mementoes of Sofia's he'd take with him. Sara had put Dani to bed shortly after José retired to his room, and she'd sat on the comforter and listened to her daughter's adventure at the Dairy Queen and what Cruz had said he'd do if Tanner kept teasing Dani at school. Although she'd laughed, Sara couldn't help but wish Cruz could be there for Dani for real when she had trouble at school. Sara worried that having only one parent would force Dani to grow up faster than a little girl her age should. She didn't want Tony's sense-less murder to not only steal Dani's father from her, but also her childhood.

Sara paused outside the barn doors and smoothed a hand over her hair. Tomorrow she'd put on a brave face and say goodbye to Cruz. But tonight she wanted to thank him in private for all his help.

You want more than that.

Ignoring the voice in her head, she entered the struc-ture. "Are you finished?"

Cruz kept his back to her as he hoisted a hay bale onto his shoulder and walked it to the pile he'd built in the back corner. He deposited the bale on top of the others, then faced her. Neither spoke.

What was there to say? Everything she felt for Cruz was there in her eyes and she didn't bother hiding it. She couldn't bear the thought of saying goodbye to him for good. She wanted him to promise her that he'd keep in touch. That he'd visit her and Dani in Albuquerque. Call her once in a while so she could hear his voice and know that he was okay. But he wouldn't. Their weeks together were a one-time thing and that was all it would ever be.

With her eyes she willed him to come closer. His lazy-hipped stride made her pulse race. He stopped in front of her and trailed his fingertips down her cheek and neck, stopping at her collarbone. She shivered.

"I'll miss you, Sara Mendez."

"I'll miss you more." She caressed his jaw.

"This is a bad idea."

"I've run out of good ideas." She lifted her mouth to his and held her breath, hoping he wouldn't push her away. In the next breath his lips covered hers and she gave herself over to his gentle care. He made her yearn for more, then answered her silent pleas by deepening the kiss. This was their final goodbye and the desperation tugging at her soul refused to settle for slow and easy. She shoved her fingers through his hair, then pressed herself against him until he gathered her close—close enough for her to feel how much he wanted her.

If they found a way to be together, would the fire between them always burn this hot? Wondering was a waste of time. Her first priority was her family, but this night belonged to her. His hands found her breasts, his touch drawing a moan from deep inside her. She reached for his belt, her fingers fumbling with the buckle until his hand trapped hers against the leather.

"Wait," he said.

"I don't want to wait."

Holding her face, he rested his forehead against hers. "I wish…"

"What?"

"Nothing." He kissed her as he walked her backward into a stall filled with fresh hay.

Time passed in a blur. Hands and mouths touched and kissed while clothes were pushed out of the way to make room for more touching and more kissing.

When they stopped moving and only their harsh breath echoed around them, Sara battled tears. She didn't want Cruz to see her cry. He'd feel guilty and that wasn't fair since she'd come to him asking for this. She buried her face in the crook of his neck and hugged him hard, then shrugged into her clothes and left the barn. She headed straight for her room, where she threw herself across the bed and bawled like a baby.

Cruz stood in the darkened doorway of the barn, staring at the house. He touched the wetness on his neck. He'd never felt such a strong emotion for anyone in his life. Had he fallen in love with Sara? Did he even know what love was? If the hollow feeling that had attacked him after she fled the stall was any indication, then he'd definitely fallen in love with her.

"Is everything loaded?" Cruz asked Sara Saturday morning. He, Sara and José had risen at dawn to pack the remaining items in the trailer.

"I think so." Sara glanced at José, who searched through his toolbox. "Which rodeo are you riding in this afternoon?"

"Red Rock." He was heading west, and they were traveling north.

"I hope it goes well."

He smiled. "I doubt it will."

"One of these times the judges will have to give you a fair score."

He figured he could rodeo the rest of his life and never earn a score in the eighties. He had no one to blame but himself and the choices he'd made in the past. What did it matter? Sara and Dani were moving on and he had to make decisions about his future. Rodeoing forever wasn't in the cards.

"Did you get all your things from the trailer?" she asked.

He nodded.

"If rodeoing doesn't work out, you're welcome to use the trailer. José would be glad to have someone watching over the property."

Living in Papago Springs without Sara would be torture. It was best to make a clean break from the town. "Thanks, but I won't be coming back."

He hated goodbyes—maybe because this was the first one he'd actually experienced. After the jury had handed him a guilty verdict, he hadn't had the chance to say goodbye to anyone before they'd whisked him from the courtroom and returned him to jail.

"You sure you can handle the trailer?" The rental business had given Sara a larger trailer than she'd asked for because the smaller size she'd reserved hadn't been delivered to the lot.

"We'll take our time. It's a straight shot up Highway 25."

"Watch out for the wind."

"We will."

José joined them and held out his hand to Cruz. After they shook he said, "Thank you for helping me fix up the place."

"Sure."

José returned inside the house and Cruz said, "I better hit the road."

"Let me wake Dani. She'll be upset if she doesn't get a chance to say goodbye."

He held out his hands and backed up a step. "Let

her sleep. We said goodbye last night." The little pip-squeak had given him a hug and just about broken his heart when she'd asked him to come visit her in Albuquerque.

He glanced at the house and spotted José spying in the window. Even though Cruz yearned to kiss Sara goodbye, he held back.

"Keep this." She handed him a business card. "It's the number for the clinic I work at. If you ever visit Albuquerque, call me and we can meet for dinner."

He shoved the card in his jeans pocket. "Will you do me a favor?" he asked.

"What's that?"

"Smile when I drive away."

Her eyes welled with tears and when one escaped he caught the tiny droplet with the pad of his thumb. "When I look in the rearview mirror, the last thing I want to see is your smile."

"Okay."

Cruz walked to his truck, then paused after he opened the door and looked at her. "I'll never forget you, Sara Mendez." He slid behind the wheel, then fumbled with the keys when his hand started shaking. He finally shoved the key into the ignition and fired up the motor. Making sure he didn't look her way, he backed onto the road and shifted into Drive. When he finally got the courage to look in the mirror, Sara was smiling.

He ignored the burning sensation in his eyes and focused on the black ribbon of asphalt pulling his tires farther and farther away from Papago Springs and the one person he wanted to spend the rest of his life with.

Chapter Eleven

Forty miles outside of Red Rock, New Mexico, Cruz pulled off the road and stared out the windshield. He couldn't get the image of Sara towing the trailer out of his mind. His gut clenched when he pictured her having trouble controlling the SUV.

You can't go to Albuquerque. You'll violate your probation.

A sweat broke out across his brow. He'd waited twelve years to be released from that hellhole, and if he got caught in Albuquerque his taste of freedom would abruptly end. But having to live with the knowledge that something had happened to Sara, Dani and José because he hadn't been there to help would be worse than another lifetime behind bars.

He shifted into Drive, checked his mirrors, then turned the truck around and headed to Papago Springs. Sara had an hour's lead on him, but he figured she'd be driving below the speed limit and he'd easily catch them. He pressed the accelerator to the floor, then eased up when the speedometer hit eighty. Without a valid driver's license he couldn't afford to be pulled over by the highway patrol. When he drove into Papago Springs it was 10:30 a.m. Sara's car and José's truck were gone. He continued north, hoping to catch a glimpse of them within an hour.

Keeping his eyes peeled, he passed three horse trailers and one tractor but no sign of a white SUV or José's battered pickup.

After another fifteen miles Cruz slowed down to navigate a sharp curve in the road that hugged an outcropping of rock. When the road straightened in front of him, he slammed on the brakes. Sara's car sat in a ditch—the trailer twenty yards away, tipped on its side, José's truck parked behind that.

Cruz's heart plummeted to his stomach as he parked on the shoulder. Where were they? He shut off the engine and hopped out, then sprinted up to the SUV and looked through the windows. The seats were empty. Same for José's vehicle. He shielded his eyes from the sun and glanced down the road—no sign of them walking for help. Had a stranger given them a ride to the nearest town?

Before Cruz had figured out his next move, a highway patrol car appeared in the distance. The squad car pulled in front of Sara's SUV, then a moment later the officer, Sara, José and Dani exited the vehicle. The knot in his stomach unraveled and Cruz felt the tension seep from his body. Thank God they were all okay.

"Mr. Cruz! Mr. Cruz!" Dani rushed toward him. "I got to ride in a police car!"

It felt as natural as breathing when Cruz bent and scooped Dani into his arms. He propped her on his hip. "Looks like your mom had some trouble with the trailer."

Dani nodded, then wiggled to get down and Cruz set her on the ground.

Sara smiled sheepishly. "I took the curve too fast and the trailer hitch broke loose."

"I'm glad no one was hurt." Cruz watched the officer check out the trailer.

"You're supposed to be in Red Rock at a rodeo," José said.

"Changed my mind and thought maybe you could use my help getting to Albuquerque."

"You should have changed your mind before you left this morning." José frowned.

"I'm here now." Cruz walked up to the officer. "Any chance you've got a rope or tie-downs in your car?"

"Rope," the officer said, leading the way to his vehicle.

Cruz waited for the officer to ask for his name, but today was his lucky day. The radio in the patrol car went off and the officer took the call. "I've got an emergency," he said, opening the trunk. "I'll swing by here in a couple of hours. Hopefully you'll be gone." He tossed the rope to Cruz.

"We'll leave the rope on the side of the road," Cruz said.

"Take it. You might need it again."

Sara thanked the officer for his help before he drove off, then asked Cruz, "Where's he going?"

"Another emergency. I need you to move your car, so I can back my truck up to the trailer. I've got a hitch on it."

"What's the rope for?" she asked.

"If I can't pull the trailer out on my own, then I'll attach the rope to José's truck and have him pull, too."

"Cruz."

"What?"

"I'm glad you came back."

Her smile squeezed his chest. "Me, too." When he got to his truck, he spoke to José. "Will you keep Dani out of the way?"

José took his granddaughter's hand and walked several yards down the road. The old man acted grumpy but Cruz sensed he was relieved to have help in this situation even if he wasn't sure what Cruz's sudden appearance meant for his daughter-in-law. He'd bet José would be more than happy to toss him ten bucks for pulling the trailer out of the ditch, then send him on his way.

Rescuing the trailer was a slow process, but he'd never been more grateful now that Shorty had gifted him his truck. The diesel engine had the power to pull the loaded trailer upright and back onto the road.

"Thanks, Cruz." Sara stopped by his side. "Between you and me, that was a little scary. I'm just glad the SUV didn't roll over."

"I'm keeping the trailer hitched to my truck."

"You're coming with us to Albuquerque?" The bright light in Sara's eyes nearly blinded him.

"I'll make sure you get there safe and sound and help you unload."

She flung her arms around his neck and hugged him. "Thank you."

He couldn't help himself—knew he shouldn't with José watching—but he buried his face against her neck. Lord, he was going to miss her. He walked off, needing to put a little distance between them. Fifteen minutes later, the group was ready to get back on the road. Cruz made Sara lead, then José followed and he brought up the rear. If the trailer was going to come loose again he didn't want Sara or José running into it.

They had two hours and fifteen minutes until they reached Albuquerque and Cruz hoped he'd be able to get in and out of the city without any trouble.

Then what?

Then he'd say a final goodbye to the family and figure out his next rodeo. And all he could hope for was that each eight seconds he stayed in the saddle brought him a little closer to figuring out what he wanted to do with his life and how he intended to move on without Sara.

The drive to Albuquerque went smoothly. They stopped once to gas up the vehicles—Sara insisted the prices were cheaper outside the city limits than inside. Cruz hadn't paid attention to gas prices when he'd lived there because he hadn't owned a car and neither had his mother.

As they drew closer to the city, traffic picked up and Cruz concentrated on his driving and not letting his attention wander. Easier said than done. The Sandia Mountains along the east side of the city reminded him of another lifetime when he'd believed he'd been invincible. A time when he hadn't thought about the future, only living in the here and now.

They entered the suburbs south of the city and Cruz thought for sure Sara would turn down one of the major streets leading into the communities, but she didn't. Her deceased husband had worked at a clinic in the barrio on the south side, but surely they hadn't lived near that area. An unsettling feeling gripped Cruz's stomach. He hadn't counted on driving through his old stomping grounds and risk being recognized by any homies from his past.

Sara drove across the Rio Grande River, which flowed through the middle of the city, and turned onto Central Avenue. Cruz knew every inch of this street and could walk it blindfolded. A quarter mile later she drove down Silver Avenue and parked in front of a small one-story home with an attached carport. He pulled into the driveway with the trailer and José parked on the street behind Sara's SUV.

The house needed some TLC—the stucco could use a fresh coat of paint and the landscaping looked scruffy. The welcome sign hanging next to the door seemed out of place with bars over the windows. The houses on the block looked the same except painted in different colors. Some had one-car garages, most didn't. There were tricycles and balls strewn across the yards and empty soda bottles and fast-food wrappers littering the street. At the end of the block three teenagers lounged on a porch and stared in their direction.

He waited outside while Sara unlocked the front door and let Dani and her grandfather into the house. "I can't believe you haven't had your car stolen or vandalized parked out here," he said when Sara returned.

"We bought the car right before Tony was killed. My neighbors were grateful for the work Tony did at the clinic. No one has bothered my house or car since his death."

No wonder she hadn't moved. She was probably safer here than anywhere in Albuquerque. "Where do you want all this stuff when I bring it inside?"

"You don't have to help unload. I'm sure you're eager to get going to…wherever." Her smile faltered.

"I'm not leaving until everything's unpacked."

"Thank you." Sara opened the padlock on the trailer and he rolled up the door. "We'll put everything in the front room for now. I'm moving Dani into my bedroom for the time being, so José's luggage can go in Dani's room and whatever else he wants in there. We'll sort through the rest later." She grabbed a box and walked it up the porch steps. José found a rock in the yard and used it to hold the door open.

Cruz took the heavier boxes into the house first. After a half hour Dani brought him a bottle of water and he sat on the front porch and took a break. While she chatted about the kids in her neighborhood, he watched a black Lincoln Town Car turn the corner and head in their direction. "Go inside, Dani." When she didn't listen, he said, "Now." Eyes wide, she ran into the house.

The Lincoln slowed and a passenger in the back-seat lowered the window. Cruz's mind flashed back to the afternoon when Emilio had been shot, and his heart stopped beating. Right then Sara stepped onto the porch and the car sped away.

"Cruz? Dani said you're mad at her." She sat next to him on the steps.

"I'm sorry. It's just that…" He swallowed hard.

"What?"

"That car." He nodded to the black vehicle driving off. "It reminded me of something that happened years ago and I panicked."

"Tell me about it."

"It's not pretty."

"That's okay. I've seen a lot of not-so-pretty things in my job."

He guessed she had. "I lived in a neighborhood not far from here. Not as nice as this block. Me and my brother, Emilio, were sitting on the front porch when a black Escalade came down the street the same time a red Lincoln pulled around the corner in front of our house." Both vehicles had lowered their windows and before Cruz's brain had registered what was about to go down, shots rang out and his brother fell backward. "They were rival gang members and they opened fire on each other's cars. Bullets flew everywhere. I shoved my brother down and covered his body with mine until I heard tires squeal and the cars drive off." He closed his eyes, but the picture of his brother's lifeless body remained vivid in his memory. "By the time the paramedics arrived, Emilio had bled out on the front porch."

"My God, I'm sorry, Cruz. That's awful." She rested her head on his shoulder. "There are too many deaths from gang violence in this city."

Cruz grasped her hand, squeezing it gently. It felt right sitting next to Sara. She made him believe he belonged by her side.

"How old was your brother?" she asked.

"Nine."

"I can't imagine losing a child. Losing Tony was difficult enough, but a child—how does a parent survive that kind of pain? Parents are supposed to protect their children from harm."

Cruz's mother hadn't been home the afternoon Emilio had died. She'd been at her usual hangout—an abandoned building a mile away from the neighborhood where a meth lab operated. She'd returned later that day high as a kite. When she saw the blood on the porch, all she'd said to Cruz was "Clean it up." It wasn't until the next morning when she'd come down from her high that she'd asked where Emilio was. In that moment Cruz had hated her with all his being. Then she'd glanced at the front door, her face going pale when she remembered the blood on the porch. "Is he dead?" she'd asked.

"The policeman said you're supposed to go to the morgue and claim his body."

His mother had grabbed her purse and left the house. Cruz had taken off, staying away from home for a week. He'd spent a couple of nights at Victor's house and a few at Alonso's before returning home. He hadn't asked what happened to Emilio's body, and his mother never said.

"You had a tough childhood, didn't you?"

His childhood was no different than that of most kids in the barrio. "My mother died of a heart attack when I was in prison." Her heart weakened by years of drug abuse.

"Do you have other siblings?"

"My mother had a daughter and another son. Different fathers than mine. I wasn't close to them. I have no idea where they are or if they even live in Albuquerque."

Sara squeezed his hand. "I'm glad nothing bad happened to you."

Prison was bad, but he knew what she meant.

"Maybe you could try to locate your siblings," she said. "I'd always wished I had a brother or sister. Tony was an only child, too. With my parents living in France, José is all the family Dani and I have."

Sara lived in a dream world if she believed Cruz

could just dial a number, reach his siblings and then enjoy a happy reunion. Chances were his brother and sister wanted nothing to do with him because he had a prison record. And if that didn't bother them, then they were likely living the type of lives he was trying to avoid.

She nudged his shoulder. "I was thinking since you didn't rodeo today that you might be able to—"

He stood, interrupting her. He knew what she was going to ask—she wanted him to stay. First, it would be for the night, then the next day and the next and then goodbye would be impossible. "What do you say we go out for a bite to eat after we finish unloading?"

"Just the two of us?" she asked.

"Yeah."

"I'm dying to eat at one of my favorite restaurants."

"Where's that?"

"A little Szechuan place a few blocks away. I love their kung pao chicken."

"I've never eaten Szechuan, but I'm willing to try it."

Her eyes sparkled. "Great. I better head inside and get working so we don't end up eating at ten o'clock tonight."

As soon as Sara left the porch, he continued unloading the trailer. He'd stick around long enough to have dinner, then he'd put as many miles as possible between him and Albuquerque.

"How come I can't go along?" Dani sat on the bed, playing with Sara's jewelry.

"Because." Sara intended to talk Cruz into staying in Albuquerque.

"Is Mr. Cruz gonna come back and see us?"

"I hope so, honey." If she couldn't convince him to stick around longer, she wanted him to promise he'd come back and visit. She believed with all her heart that what they'd shared in the short time they'd known each other was special. Never had she believed she'd meet a man who'd just gotten out of prison and then connect with him in the way she'd bonded with Cruz. No matter what anyone said about him, deep down inside he was a good man.

"I bet Daddy would like Mr. Cruz."

Sara's fingers froze on the zipper of her sundress. She was surprised Dani had brought up her father. She zipped her dress, then sat on the bed and brushed her daughter's bangs off her forehead. "Do you think about Daddy often?"

Dani shook her head. "No." Then her eyes welled with tears.

Sara hugged her. "What is it?"

"All my friends have daddies."

"Don't give up hope. One day another daddy might come into your life."

"I want Mr. Cruz to be my daddy."

Sara heard a noise outside the room and glanced at the doorway. José stood in the hall staring at them, his face pasty-white. After a second he walked off, but Sara guessed he'd overheard Dani. She hugged her daughter harder. "Life isn't always fair, honey. We might have to wait a long time for someone special to come along."

"I hope I don't have to wait for a daddy forever."

"Me, too." Sara released Dani, then stood in front of the mirror and put on her lip gloss. "Be good for

Papa tonight. He's a little sad, too, because he had to leave the cantina."

"We can watch a movie," Dani said.

"That's a great idea."

Dani slid off the bed and left the room. "Papa?" she called out. "Will you watch a movie…" Her voice faded after she entered the kitchen.

With a last glance in the mirror, Sara went outside to see if Cruz had finished unloading. She assumed he'd want to clean up before eating out. While he showered she'd make supper for José and Dani. Then she'd have her work cut out for her convincing Cruz to stay.

"I THOUGHT WE'D WALK," Sara said when she and Cruz descended the porch steps.

"I'm not sure that's such a good idea." Walking at night was risky in the barrio. There weren't enough cops to patrol all the neighborhoods. When he'd hung out with his homies he hadn't carried a gun, but he had carried a knife. Tonight he had no protection and no way to defend Sara—except with his fists—if they got jumped. The only thing in his pocket was money, which made him a target no matter how confident Sara was that nothing would happen to them in the two blocks they had to walk to the restaurant.

"This is a decent neighborhood. Mostly families."

He made sure he walked on the side facing the street, then held Sara's hand.

"Cruz?"

"What?"

"Don't get me wrong." She smiled. "I'm not complaining for the help on the road earlier today…but why did you come back?"

When he didn't answer right away, her smile faded but the light remained in her eyes—a glimmer of hope that he'd returned to offer her more than a helping hand. He knew she wanted him to say he'd changed his mind about heading down the road. "I was worried that something might happen. I wanted to make sure you arrived in Albuquerque safely."

And I didn't want to say goodbye.

They reached the corner and waited for a car to pass before crossing the street. "The China Noodle House is right around that corner." She pointed down the block.

Cruz had driven through this area from time to time growing up, but hadn't eaten at any of the ethnic restaurants. His diet had consisted of fast food and convenience-store hot dogs. His mother had rarely cooked a meal. If they were lucky, they might have found a box of cereal in the cupboard and milk in the fridge.

"When do you go back to work?" he asked.

"Monday. Now that I don't have to worry about day care, I might switch to the swing shift. I don't like getting off work late at night, but it pays more."

He didn't like the idea of Sara driving home from the clinic in the dark by herself. When they rounded the corner, Cruz's internal alarm went off. He grabbed Sara's arm and tugged her into the doorway of the restaurant seconds before a gunshot echoed through the air.

Sara gasped and Cruz pressed her farther into the shadows behind him. His eyes roamed up and down the block and into doorways, but he saw no one with a gun. Then he glanced up at the apartments above the businesses. A man leaned out a window waving a gun.

"Don't move," he whispered, positioning his body in front of hers. The gunman hadn't looked their way yet, but if he did they'd be in his direct line of sight. Before he had a chance to warn Sara not to open the restaurant door and draw attention to them, she did just that. The shooter's gun swung toward them, but instead of feeling a bullet slam into him, Cruz heard, "Rivera? Cruz Rivera? Is that you, homie?"

"You know that man?" Sara whispered.

Cruz had no idea who the guy was, but chances were good that he'd known him twelve years ago when he'd been running the streets.

"Get inside," he said.

Sara did as he asked and once he knew she was safe, he stepped into the light.

"Well, shit, Rivera! When did you get out of the big house?"

Cruz didn't care to draw attention to himself, but he refused to shout back and forth with the man. He crossed the street and stood below the open window. "I got out a few weeks ago. I'm just passing through town."

"Where're you living?"

Cruz still didn't recognize the guy, but then after a while they all looked the same—tattoos, baggy clothes and guns. He heard a siren in the distance and figured he'd better get in the restaurant before the cops stopped him and discovered he was violating his parole.

"Don't kill anyone." Cruz hustled across the street. Inside the restaurant he found Sara waiting for him. She looked pale and shaken. Tonight's incident reminded him once again why he could never be with her.

"Who was that man?" she asked.

"A gangbanger."

"He knew you."

Cruz nodded. He might as well tell her the truth. She needed to know who he really was. "I was pledging a gang right before I went to prison."

She swallowed hard. "Which one?"

"The Los Locos."

Her eyes rounded in shock. "I've lost my appetite." She went for the door but Cruz blocked her path.

"Wait until things settle down outside."

"Why? I just want to go home."

"If the police stop to question me, they'll learn I've violated my parole by coming to Albuquerque." He didn't need to explain what that meant. The turmoil in Sara's eyes told him she understood that if they walked out the door now, he might end up back in prison.

"I guess I could eat something."

Chapter Twelve

Sara picked at her food, hardly tasting the dish. She didn't know what to think after learning that Cruz had been associated with the Los Locos gang—the thugs who'd killed her husband. He'd been in prison and hadn't been a member of the gang at the time Tony had been shot, but she couldn't wrap her head around the role fate was playing in her life. Why had the powers that be guided Cruz to Papago Springs after her husband's senseless death?

Why had fate allowed her to get close to Cruz and… No, she refused to say the words in her mind. She couldn't fall in love with him. Never mind that her feelings for him had slipped past caring and had been racing toward head-over-heels when he'd rescued them on the side of the road today. In the span of seven hours she'd gone from thinking they had a chance to be together, to they didn't have a chance in hell now that she knew he'd been associated with the Los Locos.

She glanced at Cruz across the table—he wasn't eating, either. "You should have gone to the rodeo." She would have been better off never learning about his association with the gang. She would have at least had hope that maybe one day they might find their way back to each other. Now even her hope had been dashed.

"I should have." The pain in his eyes stole her breath. "But I had to be sure all of you made it here safely."

"Can I ask why it's a violation of your parole to be in Albuquerque?"

"My parole officer believes I'll be less tempted to become involved in gangs."

"Did you plan on looking up old friends while you were here?" He winced and she regretted her question.

"No. I'd planned to see that you made it home, then leave."

He didn't have to tell her that he intended to hit the road tonight as soon as they returned to the house.

"I'm sorry I didn't say anything before," he said.

"Before...?"

"I moved my things into the trailer."

She understood his reasoning for keeping his past to himself, but it hurt that he hadn't mentioned his gang affiliation once he'd learned how Tony had been killed.

The waitress stopped by their table to refill their water glasses. She nodded to the half-eaten meals. "Is there something the matter with your food?"

"No," Sara said. "I'm not as hungry as I thought."

The woman nodded and walked off.

She struggled for something else to say, but what was the use? It was over between them—over before their relationship had had a chance to grow.

He tossed his napkin on his plate. "Ready?"

She scooted her chair back and he left two twenties on the table, then escorted her to the door. Outside the street was quiet and there were no patrol cars on the scene.

They walked the two blocks back to her house in silence. When they reached the front porch, Cruz stayed on the sidewalk while she climbed the porch steps. Sara's throat ached. "Do you want to say goodbye to Dani and José?"

He shook his head. "It's better if I just leave."

So then why didn't he turn around and walk away? Why did he just stand there and stare at her with pleading eyes?

"Sara." He shoved a hand through his hair, which hadn't been cut since he'd shown up in Papago Springs. The shaggier style made him look reckless and daring and so darn sexy. "I'm sorry."

"For what?" He'd made no promises. He'd done nothing she hadn't wanted him to do. He'd been kind and patient with Dani and respectful toward José. He'd been perfect.

"For not being good enough for you."

A sharp pain sliced through her heart.

"I wish I could have been anybody else but me when we met."

I fell in love with you.

He walked to his truck, then paused after opening the door. "I won't forget you, Sara."

And she'd never be able to forget him.

He slid behind the wheel and drove off. She stood on the porch and watched until his taillights turned the corner and disappeared from sight. The door creaked open behind her.

"Where's Cruz going?" José asked.

"He left."

"I can see that. When is he coming back?"

She faced her father-in-law. "He's not." *Are you*

happy now that he's no longer a threat to your son's widow? She brushed past him and entered the house. Dani said something to her when she walked through the living room but she didn't catch the words. She went straight to her room and locked the door behind her, then sank onto the bed. Only then did she let the tears fall.

A torrent of water leaked from her eyes—two years of emotions bottled up inside her broke free. Since her husband's death she'd been the strong one in the family, putting on a brave face and reassuring everyone that they'd be okay. Cruz's leaving had broken the dam and this time she was unable to contain the fear, hurt and sadness that she'd buried inside her for so long.

CRUZ'S STOMACH GROWLED LOUDLY. He'd driven straight to Interstate 25 after leaving Sara's—bypassing his old neighborhood. He'd had no desire to see the run-down home he'd grown up in. The turnoff for Interstate 40 came up, and without thinking he took the exit and headed northwest. As he put mile after mile between him and the city, he decided he'd never be able to return—even if they lifted the parole restriction. It would be too painful to live or visit the place knowing Sara was there.

He drove for over an hour before his growling stomach forced him to stop at a gas station convenience store.

"Howdy," the elderly man behind the counter greeted Cruz. "If you're looking for a restroom, you'll have to go farther down the road to the truck stop. Got a plumber coming out tomorrow to see about fixing the toilet."

Cruz studied the refrigerated drinks, then selected a bottle of water and helped himself to a shriveled-up hot dog from beneath the heat lamp.

"I'll charge you half price for the dog."

Cruz handed over a five-dollar bill, then dropped his change into the charity box next to the register.

"Drive careful," the old man said.

"Thanks." Cruz ate the hot dog in the truck and stared out the windshield. The last thing he wanted to do was compete in another rodeo. After he finished his meal, he went back into the store. The old guy looked up—this time his smile was hesitant, as if he worried Cruz had returned to rob him.

"You happen to know how I might get to the Juan Alvarez Ranch for Boys from here?"

"Sure do. You got a kid there?"

"A friend works there."

"Take the next exit, then turn left over the highway. It's about twenty miles. You'll see a sign before the entrance. Gates probably locked this late at night. Might have to wait until tomorrow morning to get in."

"Thanks." Forty minutes later, Cruz pulled onto the shoulder of the road and parked next to the impressive iron gates. He approved of the bucking bronc logo with the words *Juan Alvarez Ranch* inside the iron circle. It was midnight—too late for a social call. He turned off the engine and unrolled the windows. It was pitch-black outside with only a few stars in the sky for light. Slouching in his seat, he closed his eyes, then opened them wide when Sara's pretty face floated through his mind.

He had no idea what he was going to say to Fitzgerald tomorrow. All he knew was that he had nowhere to go except the circuit, and the thought of climbing onto another bronc and riding in front of a silent crowd had about as much appeal as getting a tooth pulled without Novocain.

He just hoped Shorty would forgive him for bailing out early.

SARA STOPPED AT the nurses' station in the children's clinic to look up a patient's record when Janet, the shift manager, pointed over her shoulder.

"He's been waiting almost an hour for you."

Sara's heart flipped upside down in her chest and she spun. As soon as she recognized that it was her father-in-law and not Cruz sitting in the waiting area, the organ slowed to a dull thud. She hurried to the lounge. "Is something wrong, José? Is it Dani?"

He shook his head. "Dani is fine. I dropped her off at the school this morning."

Sara had been working overtime the past two weeks. The money was great and by the time she hit the sack she was exhausted and slept like the dead—not even dreaming, which was a good thing since she couldn't get Cruz out of her head during the day. "Something must be on your mind if you stopped by the hospital."

"We need to talk."

"We can talk when I get home."

He scowled.

"What?" Sometimes her father-in-law exasperated her.

"You're avoiding me. I want to know why."

José was being contrary. "How can I avoid you when we live under the same roof?" she asked.

"You've been working long hours ever since Cruz left town."

A coworker stared at them and Sara decided to move her conversation with José elsewhere. "Let's talk outside." She led the way to an outdoor patio used by patients and staff. There was plenty of shade near the benches so she chose one, then sat and waited for him to speak.

"You've changed since Rivera left."

"You're imagining things." Was he trying to pick a fight so she'd suggest he move back to Papago Springs? "Are you unhappy living with Dani and me?"

"No!"

Good. Dani loved having her grandfather to come home to after preschool and was already chatting with him about walking together to kindergarten in the fall.

"It's you that is unhappy," he said. "You don't laugh or smile anymore and you get short-tempered with Dani."

Sara rubbed her brow. She might have convinced herself she was fine, but obviously her father-in-law saw through her. "I'm getting used to being back at work and the overtime leaves me tired."

"Then don't work the extra hours. I'm giving you rent money. Why do you need to work more?"

She blinked away the tears that were always ready to fall. She wasn't aware that she was wringing her hands until José grasped them in his. "Tell me. I can't help you unless I know what's bothering you."

She forced a smile. "I wish it was that simple, but this can't be fixed." The hurt in José's gaze punched her in the stomach. She thought she was protecting him from the truth, but she was making things worse.

"Do you want me to move back to Papago Springs?"

Was he kidding? The look on his face told her he was stubborn enough to pack his bags and leave if she didn't come clean. "No, I don't want you to leave. I just miss Cruz." That was the truth. A better truth than telling him about Cruz's involvement with the gang that had killed José's son.

José stared unseeingly at the water fountain across the patio. He didn't have to say a word—she knew what was going through his mind... How could the wife of his deceased son befriend an ex-con? How could Sara have let Cruz be with his grandchild? Take Dani for ice cream alone in his truck?

This was why Sara could never be with Cruz—she couldn't betray her father-in-law. It was a no-win situation and she couldn't pick between the two men.

"Do you love Cruz?" José's voice broke when he asked the question.

"It doesn't matter." If she chose to be with Cruz, Dani would lose a grandfather and her daughter had already lost a father.

"I need to think about this."

"There's nothing to think about. Cruz is gone and he's not coming back."

José stared into Sara's eyes and she did her best not to flinch, but she feared he could see into her soul.

"You fell in love with him."

She glanced at her watch. "I have to get back to work."

"Sara—"

"I promise I won't work any more overtime." She left the patio and stepped into the first elevator that opened. Luckily José hadn't followed her. She had six hours left to cherish the memories of her time with

Cruz. When she got home tonight she intended to put him behind her for good.

Six hours flew by and a little after ten-thirty that evening, Sara walked into her house to find José waiting up for her. Instead of rushing off to her room, she sat down and asked, "How was Dani today?"

"Cranky."

"Why's that?"

"She'd rather have you tuck her into bed at night."

Sara felt a twinge of shame for ignoring her daughter. "I'll be home by supper time tomorrow." She motioned to the kitchen doorway. "Would you like a cup of tea?"

"No. I'm going away this weekend."

"With who?"

"Myself."

"Where?"

"I don't know yet."

This was crazy. Had the move to Albuquerque messed with his brain? "I know you must be bored all day waiting for Dani to get out of school. I'll speak with Mrs. Garcia down the street. She's active in her church and the local food pantry. Maybe they could use the services of a great cook for one of their fundraisers or the soup kitchen."

"I don't want to cook for other people."

Sara knew that was a lie. Good grief, when he made supper for the three of them there were leftovers for days afterward. He missed cooking and socializing with people who'd stopped in at the cantina. Once he got involved in the community she was sure he'd settle in and enjoy Albuquerque.

"I'll be gone for a couple of days. No longer than that."

"You're serious, aren't you?"

"Think I'll turn in." He walked off muttering, "There's leftover enchiladas if you're hungry."

Sara helped herself to an enchilada even though she wasn't hungry. Hopefully when the weekend arrived, José would forget taking a trip to who knew where.

Fat chance. The rest of the week rolled by and Saturday morning, José headed for the front door carrying an overnight bag. "I'll call you when I get there."

"Get where?" she asked, alarmed.

"Wherever I end up."

She followed him outside to his truck where he set the bag in the backseat. "What if something happens to you? How will I know where to send the police looking?"

"I've got my cell phone. If I have any trouble, I'll call." He got into the truck, started the engine and drove off without a wave or smile or glance in his side mirrors.

Sara stood on the curb for almost ten minutes wondering what to do. Should she wake Dani and go after him? Call the police now, and tell them her father-in-law was suffering a nervous breakdown and should be brought back home?

This was all her fault. If she hadn't wallowed in her own self-pity after Cruz had taken off, she would have noticed José wasn't adjusting well to the move. She headed into the house, deciding she'd give him his two-day vacation and then if he didn't return, she'd send the National Guard after him.

"THOUGHT I MIGHT find you in here."

Cruz looked up from the cot he sat on in the bunk-house. Fitzgerald stood in the doorway, his expression sober. After a moment he stepped farther into the room and helped himself to a seat at the picnic table in the kitchen area.

"I didn't realize how much he meant to me until I found out he was dead." Cruz held Shorty's hat in his hand and stared at the sweaty crown.

"He talked about you constantly."

"I wish I hadn't banned him from visiting me in prison." Shorty had been as close to a grandfather as Cruz had ever had.

"Even if you'd have granted him visitation, I wouldn't have let him see you," Fitzgerald said.

The answer stung. "Why?"

"Because I didn't want his last memory of you to be a conversation through a glass window."

"You knew he was sick?"

"Maria suspected something was wrong long before I did. She encouraged him to see a doctor, but he refused. He told her it was God's business when it was his time to go and not something he should interfere with."

"That sounds like Shorty." Cruz's smile trembled. "Was he chewing and spitting up to the end?" When Cruz and his friends had first met Shorty, the old man had impressed them by how far he could spit tobacco juice.

"He never gave up his chew, not even at the end when it made him nauseous." Fitzgerald cleared his throat. "It was a blessing when he suffered the heart attack and didn't suffer from the cancer anymore." He waved a hand in the air. "You've been here a couple of days now. You want to talk about it?"

Cruz was thirty-one years old, but he felt as if he were eighteen again, having to answer for his actions. He wondered if that feeling would ever go away, or if it would be something that stuck with him the rest of his life. "There's not much to talk about."

His mentor chuckled. "Let's see. You almost landed in juvenile detention when you were seventeen for tagging public property. You lost your brother to gang violence when you were just kids. Your father killed a man in self-defense and is still in prison. Your mother died of a heart attack. You took the fall for your best friend and ended up in prison yourself. You're one of the best bronc riders in the country, unbeknownst to the current ranked rodeo cowboys. And you're in love with a woman you don't believe you're good enough for. How about you pick one of the above and we can chat about that."

"How did you know I fell in love with Sara?"

"I might be older than you, but I recognized your feelings for her. It was there in your voice and in the way you looked at her. So why aren't you with Sara?"

"Isn't it obvious? I'm an ex-con. She and her daughter deserve better than a jailbird. If we were together, I'd cause them nothing but misery. The kids at school would tease Dani if they found out I'd been in prison, and the teachers would be terrified of me." He poked himself in the chest. "I know what it's like to listen to others mock your mother and father. I don't wish that on anyone, especially a sweet little girl like Dani."

"I can see where Sara and Dani might face some

prejudice. Have you thought about the three of you living somewhere else?"

"Sara's got a good job in Albuquerque. I can't ask her to leave."

"What does she do?"

"She's a pediatric nurse. Works at a children's clinic."

Fitzgerald's stare grew thoughtful. "She could find a job working with kids just about anywhere, I'd think."

He wasn't bringing up anything Cruz hadn't thought about already. The only problem was that a fresh start somewhere new didn't change Cruz's past or who he'd been or was now. Sooner or later, word would get out that he'd spent time in jail, and then suddenly the friends Dani made at school would disappear and neighbors would quit inviting them over for barbecues and Sara would be ostracized at her job or by the mothers at school.

And Fitzgerald was forgetting one important point. "What am I going to do to support them?" He had pride—not much after his stint in prison—but he refused to allow a woman to pay his way. "I tried to go back on the circuit. That's what Shorty wanted, but I can't keep beating a dead horse."

"Your competition giving you a hard time?"

Cruz nodded. "I can take their ridicule, but the fact that I won clear as day but the judges scored me low is more than I can handle. The rodeo community doesn't believe I deserve to win or even compete because of my prison record. Never mind that I once wanted to win a national title, I couldn't even make a living at rodeo the way things are now."

"Ever thought about coaching a new generation of bronc riders?"

"What do you mean, 'coach'?"

"You've been hiding in your room since you got here. Why don't you come with me and I'll give you a tour of the ranch. Show you what we're doing here."

Fitzgerald was right. Cruz couldn't feel sorry for himself forever. No matter that things didn't work out between him and Sara, she wouldn't want him to fall back into his old ways. Out of respect for her, he'd face the future—whatever it held for him—and make the best of it. He grabbed his hat and stood. "Let's go."

Fitzgerald escorted Cruz through a series of barns on the property and introduced him to the ranch hands who cared for the horses. "Do you grow your own hay or buy it?" Cruz asked after they'd left the hay barn.

"Mostly we grow it. Depends on the weather each year. Six years ago we had a drought and I spent a lot of money on grain."

Grain was expensive, but Fitzgerald came from money and lots of it, so Cruz doubted they'd suffered any hardships. "Does your family still race horses?"

"Yep. After my father passed away—"

"I didn't know. I'm sorry."

"Thanks. My mother talked about selling the horse farm and moving out here to the ranch with us, but my sister wouldn't let her. Bree and her husband invested in a horse named Strawberry Fields, and the colt won several events and brought in the money needed to keep the farm going."

"You ever miss your old life?"

"You mean rodeoing?"

Cruz nodded.

"Sometimes. I watch the young kids busting broncs and every once in a while I get the itch to hop on for a go-round." He chuckled. "Then I fall on my ass and decided my best days in rodeo are behind me."

They stopped at Fitzgerald's truck. "Hop in and I'll drive you out to the school."

"School?"

"Yep. We built a school on the property and every morning the kids ride a bus out to the building."

"Who drives the bus?"

"Yours truly."

The drive to the school took five minutes. The building was nestled among a stand of trees. "This is real nice."

"We've got twenty-two boys staying here right now, and three girls."

"When did you start taking in girls?"

"When Judge Hamel called and read me the riot act."

"Judge Hamel cares about kids."

Fitzgerald busted up laughing. "I recall you didn't think too highly of the woman when she sentenced you to do community service at the Gateway Ranch."

Cruz grinned, and they hopped out of the truck. "Maria won't mind the interruption." Before Cruz had a chance to object, the school door opened and he was escorted inside.

The classroom went quiet and Maria stopped writing on the whiteboard. Her eyes widened, then welled with tears when she saw Cruz.

"Aw, jeez, Ms. Alvarez, don't cry." Before Cruz realized what he was doing, he rushed to the front of the classroom and hugged his former teacher.

He was surprised by the fierceness of her hug and how it made him feel as if he'd come home. Maria was the mother he'd never had and always wished for.

She released him and smiled at the class. "Kids, this is Cruz Rivera. One of my first students."

Cruz nodded to the teens who stared at him with blank looks.

"When did you get here?" she asked.

"A short while ago."

"You're not leaving soon, are you?" she asked.

"No. I'll hang around." For however long it took him to figure out his future.

"Good. I'll see you at supper."

"You might see him before that." Fitzgerald spoke to the class. "Mr. Rivera is an accomplished bronc buster. For those of you having trouble with spurring when you come out of the gate—" he nodded to Cruz "—this is your man. No one spurs better. As soon as you finish your homework today, head out to the corral and Mr. Rivera will give you some tips."

They left the school and as soon as the door shut behind them, Cruz said, "Why'd you say I'd help them?"

"Because they need help and you're just the man to give it to them."

Cruz didn't think he could help anyone, but he felt a surge of pride that the man he'd once idolized still believed in him. The good feeling didn't last long. Even if he found a purpose in life, the empty feeling in his heart would never go away if he couldn't be with Sara.

Chapter Thirteen

"What's the matter with you, Sara?" Linda, a coworker, asked when Sara checked her phone at work for the umpteenth time.

"My father-in-law took off."

"What do you mean, 'took off'?" Linda shuffled through the patient folders lying in a stack at the nurses' station.

"He said he was going away for a couple of days. I thought maybe he was homesick and he wanted to return to Papago Springs, but when I asked him if those were his plans, he said no."

"So where's he headed, then?"

"He wouldn't say. He just told me to make arrangements for someone to watch Dani while I worked."

"He didn't give you much notice."

Sara shoved her phone into her pocket. "I thought he'd call and tell me where he went." Or how he was. For all she knew, José had driven off the road and was lying in a ditch.

"If you don't hear from him by the time your shift ends, then leave a voice mail threatening to file a missing-persons report."

"I just might do that." She perused a patient chart.

"Benji didn't eat much for lunch again." The little boy had had an emergency appendectomy two days ago. Sara suspected he missed his dog, Buddy. "I phoned his parents and asked them to bring Benji's dog with them when they come to visit." Hopefully seeing his pal again would lift the little boy's spirits.

"I'll keep an eye out for his furry little friend." Linda left the station to check on a patient.

"Hey, Benji," Sara said when she entered the eight-year-old's room. His roommate, Sam, had gone home that morning, so Benji had the place to himself. "Feeling hungry yet?" He shook his head. She pulled out her stethoscope and listened to his lungs. "All clear."

She placed a notepad and box of crayons on his lap. "My daughter, Dani, has always wanted a dog."

"That's a weird name for a girl."

"*Dani* is short for *Daniella*." Sara nodded to the crayons. "She'd love to see a picture of Buddy."

"How come she can't have a dog?"

"I work all day and Dani is at school. There's no one at home to take care of a dog." Until now. If José made up his mind to live with them permanently, maybe she could talk him into letting Dani pick out a puppy.

"My mom takes care of Buddy when I'm in school."

"I bet Buddy misses you and wonders where you are," she said. "Maybe you could draw a picture of yourself and have your mother take it home to Buddy."

Benji's eyes brightened at the suggestion and he opened the box of crayons. Right then a text message beeped on her phone. Buddy had arrived. "I have a surprise for you."

"What?"

"We're going out on the patio for some fresh air."

"I don't want to go outside."

"You have a special visitor waiting for you," she said.

"Who?"

"Buddy."

Benji threw back the covers and was halfway out of the bed before he winced and cried out.

"Not so fast, young man. You're still sore from the operation." She helped Benji into a wheelchair and then wheeled him outside. He shouted Buddy's name as soon as he saw the dog. Buddy's ears twitched, then the Great Dane let out a loud woof when he recognized Benji. The dog loped across the patio, skidding to a stop in front of his master. As if the dog knew Benji's health was frail, he lowered his massive head and rested it in Benji's lap.

Tears filled Sara's eyes at the precious picture boy and dog made. As soon as she figured out what was going on with José, she'd take Dani puppy shopping. Maybe a new dog would help them all move on from their time with Cruz.

Sara escaped the patio for a few minutes, then returned with a lunch tray and handed it to Benji's mother. "I bet Buddy will help Benji eat today."

Benji's mother nodded and a few seconds later, Benji was eating his oatmeal. Leaving the family alone, Sara returned inside and checked on her next patient.

Three hours later, Linda caught Sara in the hallway and whispered, "José left a message for you at the nurses' station." She disappeared before Sara could question her. Why had José called the nurses' station and not her cell phone?

"This message is for Sara Mendez. Tell her José will be home late tomorrow. Thank you."

He couldn't have said where he'd gone? The more Sara thought about it, the more she believed he'd returned to Papago Springs. Maybe he'd wanted to pick up a few more of his things or just check on the place. Or maybe Sofia's memory had called him home.

Had she been selfish in wanting her father-in-law to live with her and Dani? What was she going to do if he decided to return to the cantina? She couldn't drive down there to check on him every weekend. They had to find a solution that made everyone happy—if only Sara knew what that was.

"Lean back, Ben!" Cruz shouted at the teen trying to keep his seat on a bucking bronc. The boy was a quick learner and had potential, just like Fitzgerald had said.

It hadn't taken long for Fitzgerald to talk Cruz into becoming a full-time employee at the Juan Alvarez Ranch. He'd put Cruz in charge of mentoring the older boys—at-risk teens who'd been sent to the ranch as a last resort. If they didn't straighten up, the next time they got into trouble they'd end up in detention centers or jail. Cruz was doing his best to convince them not to travel down that road.

He didn't like sharing his experience in jail with the boys. He wished more than anything that his stories were about a successful rodeo career and not his time in prison—the price he'd paid for making bad choices.

The bronc reared, then came down hard enough to shake the kid loose. He flew over the horse's head and landed in the dirt with a thud. "Good ride, Ben!"

The teen crawled to his feet and limped over to Cruz. "I fell off. How is that a good ride?"

"A rodeo cowboy never falls off his horse. He gets bucked off."

"It's all the same if you land on your ass."

Cruz grinned. "We've got to work on your spurring. You're not keeping a steady rhythm and it's throwing you off balance."

"How long did it take you to learn to spur?"

"Longer than I would have liked it to. Remember, nothing worthwhile comes easy." He shook his head.

"What?"

"Nothing." Cruz wanted to laugh at himself every time he repeated a phrase Fitzgerald had once spoke to him.

"I'm not giving up. I've got the best bronc rider around to teach me." Ben smiled. "I'm taking advantage of it." He joined the other teens.

A sense of rightness filled Cruz. He appreciated the respect of the older boys—some were wary of him, because he'd spent time in jail. Others, the ones who'd been members of gangs, weren't intimidated—more in awe of him that he'd gotten out of prison and hadn't returned to his old way of life. Whatever the reason, he was happy he was needed.

"How are they doing?" Fitzgerald stopped at his side.

"With a little more work, Ben's got a chance of making it as a bronc buster."

"He reminds me of you when I first saw you ride."

It was a long time coming, but Cruz had to say it. "I'm sorry I let you and Maria down. You two were the only ones who cared about what happened to me, and I screwed up."

"We never stopped believing in you, Cruz. It just took you a little longer to come back to us."

"What do you mean, come back to you?"

"Maria always believed you'd make a good teacher."

"That's crazy. I hated school."

"Not school learning. She believes you have the ability to reach kids others can't. You've proven her right since you started working with the boys. They study you. Listen to the way you speak to others. Watch your mannerisms and how you react to situations. You're an exceptional role model. Just like Maria thought you'd be."

"You two have more faith in me than I have in myself."

"We're glad you took us up on our offer to join the team. We've needed someone like you for a long time."

Cruz didn't say anything. He liked his job. Liked working with the boys. Especially liked having a place to call home now. Even his parole officer approved of his new job and had lifted some of the parole restrictions—he was now free to travel to Albuquerque.

There wasn't an hour in the day that he didn't give a passing thought to seeing Sara again. He yearned to look at her pretty face. Know that all was well with her. And he missed little Dani. But it was best he had no contact with them. Dani deserved a father she could be proud of, not a father with a past like his. He imagined the hurt Dani would experience the first time one of her friends couldn't play at Dani's house, because the parents were afraid Dani's ex-convict father might harm their child.

"You're not happy here, are you?" Fitzgerald said.

"What do you mean?"

His boss grinned. "I know you like the job and the ranch. You get along with the other employees. But you're lonely."

Cruz chuckled, the laugh sounding odd to his own ears. "I've been pretty much alone the past twelve years."

"You miss Sara and her daughter."

Cruz sucked in a quiet breath.

"I could tell there was more going on between you two than you pretended when I stopped by Papago Springs."

"It's over."

"What happened?"

"I'd rather not talk about it." There wasn't anything anyone could do to change Cruz's past.

"Looks like you might have to talk about it anyway," Fitzgerald said. He nodded over Cruz's shoulder. "You've got a visitor."

Cruz turned from the corral and recognized José sitting in the Jeep Maria drove. *What the heck?* She stopped the vehicle a few feet away and got out, José following her.

"Look who stopped by," Maria said.

Cruz stepped forward and offered his hand. "This is a surprise, José."

Fitzgerald held out his hand. "Nice to see you again, Mr. Mendez."

How had Sara's father-in-law known where to find him?

As if Cruz had voiced the question out loud, José said, "I called your parole officer and he told me where you were working."

"Cruz will give you a tour of the ranch, Mr. Mendez." Maria signaled for her husband to follow her and the two walked off.

"Sara doesn't know where I am," José said.

The older man knew exactly what Cruz was thinking and it unnerved him.

"Are she and Dani okay?"

"Depends on what you mean by 'okay.'"

Cruz's heart thudded to a stop. "What's wrong?"

"Ever since you left, Sara's been moping around the house and working long hours at the clinic. She's hardly home for Dani—not that I mind taking care of my granddaughter. But I don't like seeing my daughter-in-law so depressed."

Cruz hated hearing that Sara was having a difficult time. He wished he could hug her and promise her that everything would be okay, but he'd probably only make things worse.

"What happened between you?" José asked.

Hadn't Sara told José that he'd been involved with the same gang that had been responsible for his son's death?

"She's in love with you, you know."

The news made Cruz both happy and sad. "I told her something about my past and she made up her mind that we couldn't be together."

"I came all this way to find out the truth and I'm not leaving until I hear it."

Cruz glanced at the group of boys who were within hearing range. "Let's take the Jeep to the pond." Fitzgerald had dug a fishing hole on the property and kept it stocked with blue gill. The ride took only a few minutes, then they got out and walked to the water's edge.

Cruz picked up a pebble and skipped it across the water's surface. "I wish I didn't have to tell you this."

"Just spit it out."

"Back in high school before I landed myself in prison, I was pledging the Los Locos gang." José didn't speak, so Cruz continued. "The same gang who shot your son." Cruz walked off, then stopped and stared into the distance.

"My daughter-in-law is special. I don't think I ever knew how special until my son died."

The old man would get no argument from Cruz. Sara was a one-of-a-kind woman.

"Sara loves and respects you, José. She won't be with me because it would betray you and your son."

José shook his head. "Sara loved my son, but Tony's first love was being a doctor. I always knew that. I was surprised she didn't leave my son after a few years, but she stayed by his side even though she and Dani played second fiddle to his career." José cleared his throat. "I can't allow her to keep sacrificing for Tony. He's gone now. And he's not coming back."

"What are you saying?"

José looked Cruz square in the eye. "Do you love my daughter-in-law?"

Cruz hadn't allowed himself to consider that word when thinking of Sara—it had been too painful. But José had made the trip to see him, and he owed him the truth. "Yes. I love Sara and Dani." He swallowed hard, bracing himself for rejection.

"You're not the man I would choose to raise my granddaughter or to be with my son's wife."

Cruz more than understood—he agreed with José.

"I'm nowhere near good enough for them. My past will only cause them pain and hurt."

"You can't escape your past, and it's bound to affect how others think of Sara and Dani and how they treat them."

"Sara's doing the right thing, José. She's protecting Dani and she was trying to protect you."

José spread his arms wide. "So how did you end up here?"

"It's a long story. You got time to hear it?"

"I've got time. I'm not leaving until tomorrow morning."

"Does Sara know you're here?"

"No. I didn't tell her where I was heading."

"She must be worried about you."

"She'll be fine." José sank to the ground and sat. "Now tell me why Maria Fitzgerald believes the sun rises and sets on you."

"Has Sara told you anything about my family?"

"Nothing."

"Are you sure you want to know? It's not good."

"Tell me everything."

"My father was a famous bull rider, but at the height of his career he got into a bar fight and killed a man in self-defense. He's still serving time in prison. After he went away, my mother fell apart and started doing drugs." Cruz couldn't believe how easy the words came. José didn't judge or interrupt. He sat quietly and listened to every detail.

"When I finally came up for parole, the warden decided he didn't want to lose his best bronc rider, so he made sure I stayed in prison. He sent a prison rapist to harass me and I swear, José, I tried to talk the man down, but he kept coming at me and I fought back. They turned on the prison camera in the room once I started swinging my fists. The fight got me another eight years behind bars."

José sat quietly, a thoughtful expression on his face. "What are your plans for the future?"

"I like it here. I like helping the boys."

"Do you intend to live here permanently?"

"Maybe. If I can help troubled teens avoid what I went through, then twelve years behind bars won't have been for nothing."

José climbed to his feet. "Let's go."

The drive to the mess hall was made in silence. When they arrived, José stood in the food line with the boys and listened to them tease each other and talk about their day. While they ate dinner, the teens entertained José with stories they'd heard about Cruz, and Ben told José that he wanted to be just like Cruz except he didn't want to spend time in jail. Cruz felt José's stare burn into him, but he kept his eyes on his plate. His stint in jail would forever be a part of who he was and could never be erased. Surely the older man understood why Sara couldn't risk being with him.

"I have a question." José spoke during a lull in conversation. "Are any of you members of the Los Locos gang?"

The boys exchanged nervous glances, then a kid named Carlos raised his hand. "My brother's a member."

"The gang is responsible for shooting my son."

"Was your son in a rival gang?" Carlos asked.

"No. He was a medical doctor who volunteered at a clinic in Albuquerque. There was a gunfight between rival gangs, and a bullet came through the clinic window and hit my son in the chest."

Dead silence filled the dining hall. The boys dropped their gazes to their plates, then Maria sat down across from José and took his hand in hers. "I knew your son, Antonio. I was in Albuquerque picking up a boy to bring to the ranch when all of a sudden he didn't feel well. I took him to the clinic before we left town. Antonio knew right away that Sergio's condition was serious and insisted I take him straight to the emergency room. He called ahead and a team of doctors were waiting for us. They rushed Sergio into surgery and repaired his torn spleen. If I hadn't stopped at the clinic that afternoon, Sergio would have probably died during the car ride to the ranch."

Maria made eye contact with each boy at the table. "This is what gang violence does. You think it's just homies shooting homies, but it's not. Innocent bystanders get caught in the crossfire and are killed, leaving their families to go on without them." She stood. "Antonio devoted his life to helping the families in that community and gangs thanked him with a bullet. Think about that the next time you find yourself missing your old way of life." Maria walked out of the mess hall.

"I'm sorry about your son, Mr. Mendez," Carlos said.

Several "me, toos" followed.

"Antonio was a good son. He cared about his patients," José said. "And now his wife and his little girl are left alone to carry on without him."

Carlos left the table and rushed out of the mess hall. Cruz went after him and found him standing by the corral.

The teen's eyes shone with tears. "What if it was a bullet from my brother's gun that killed the doctor? I remember hearing about a guy dying and the medical clinic shutting down after that."

"You'll never know, Carlos."

"I don't want to go home," the teen said. "If I do, I know my brother's gonna make me join the gang. My mom won't be able to stop him."

"You're right. There won't be much your mother can do if your brother sets his sights on you." So many kids were raised only by a mother—their fathers had abandoned them. It was a matter of survival in the barrio—each person for themselves.

"Do you think Mrs. and Mr. Fitzgerald will let me stay here forever?"

"Probably not forever, but they won't turn their backs on you, Carlos." They hadn't turned their backs on Cruz even when he'd failed them.

"I can't go home."

"You'll be stronger when you leave here. Strong enough to stand up to your brother and resist gangs. And maybe someday you'll pay it forward."

"What do you mean?"

"Maybe you'll help a kid just like you and save him from becoming a gang member."

Carlos shook his head. "A lot of good saving one kid will do."

"One kid at a time is all we can do. You're that one kid right now."

"If Maria hadn't talked the juvie judge into letting me come here, I'd be in a group home probably planning my escape."

"It's tough not to keep thinking of the past, but you have to look ahead. Because the stuff in front of you is where you can make a difference and help the most."

"What about Mr. Mendez? No one can ever make it up to him after his son was killed."

"That's true. We can't bring his son back. And he did a lot of good for the community. But you can honor his memory by staying away from gangs and helping others like yourself keep on the right path."

"What happened to you? How come you ended up in jail?"

"I was trying to help a friend from making a big mistake, but it backfired on me."

"That sucks."

"Yeah, it sucked. Big time."

"Are you gonna stay here and be a counselor now?"

"For a while. It's my chance to give back to the people who believed in me."

"I'm glad you're staying. As much as I like Mr. Fitzgerald, sometimes he doesn't understand what it's like to be in a family like mine. But you get it. You're from the barrio."

"I get it, Carlos. That's why you and I have to do better."

"I've gotta study for a test tomorrow." The kid took off, but Cruz wasn't alone. José stepped from the shadows.

"I'm leaving in the morning," he said.

Cruz nodded. Strangely enough, he'd miss the old

man. "Tell Dani and Sara… Never mind." It was best to leave well enough alone. He walked into the darkness. Alone.

Always alone.

Chapter Fourteen

"Where have you been, José?" Sara asked, startled to find him at the kitchen table drinking coffee early Saturday morning. She hadn't heard him come in last night. The idea that someone could walk into her house and she didn't hear them was another good reason to get a dog. "I've been worrying like crazy."

"I went to see someone."

"Who?"

"Cruz."

Sara's hand froze against the mug in the cupboard. She left the cup alone and turned. "Where is he?"

José frowned. "He didn't tell you where he was going when he left here?"

She shook her head.

"He's doing what he believes is best for you and Dani."

Sara's mind screamed with questions, but she held her tongue, still shocked that José had seen Cruz.

"He's working at the Juan Alvarez Ranch for Boys."

So Cruz hadn't returned to the rodeo circuit. Instead, he'd accepted Riley Fitzgerald's job offer. Part of Sara was relieved to know Cruz wasn't being subjected to ridicule and prejudice at rodeos and wasn't putting himself in situations that might result in him violating his probation, but she was also sad for him, because he'd never get the chance to fulfill a dream from his youth—becoming a saddle-bronc champion.

José's stare bore into her, his silence unnerving.

"Why did you go visit Cruz?"

"Because I can't stand to see my daughter-in-law so sad."

Sara swallowed a gasp and went to the refrigerator, pretending to search for the peanut butter while she let her father-in-law's words sink in. Obviously she'd done a horrible job hiding how much she missed Cruz.

"I know about his involvement with the Los Locos gang."

Sara stiffened.

"That's why you're not with him. Because you believe I'll view your feelings for Cruz as a betrayal of Antonio."

Darn José for seeing through her. "You're worrying for nothing. Whatever was between us…it's over. I'm focused on the future."

"Don't look me in the eye and lie," he said.

Sara swallowed hard.

"You're in love with Cruz Rivera. An ex-con who was once was associated with the gang that killed my son."

The blood drained from her face.

José studied the coffee in his mug. "I saw a different man at the ranch," he said. "A man with regrets. A man who's willing to sacrifice his happiness because he wants what's best for you and Dani. A man who believes denying himself is the only way to pay for his sins." José straightened in the chair. "But I believe there's a better way for Cruz to make up for the past and maybe, in a small way, make amends for Antonio's death and honor his memory."

Sara forced herself to speak. "What way is that?"

"Cruz Rivera can be the husband you always wished for and the father Dani never had."

"I don't understand."

"I know you were lonely married to Antonio. He told me as much. He didn't like leaving you and Dani alone, but he couldn't ignore his calling to help others."

"I always knew that." She'd understood that Tony's absences weren't because he didn't love them, but because he couldn't stop himself from helping others.

"As for my granddaughter… Antonio should have been a better father. He should have made time for Dani. My heart hurts that he went to his grave without realizing how special his daughter was."

A tear rolled down Sara's cheek.

"But that little girl down the hallway—" José pointed across the room "—she's bonded with Cruz. She feels secure and safe around him—something she never experienced with Antonio."

"Tony loved Dani, José." He just wasn't there to show it.

"But Cruz loves her, too. And he's not looking to save the world. He's looking to make peace with himself. He doesn't want to be famous or even noticed. He just wants to help troubled teens not make the same mistakes he made."

Sara was glad to hear Cruz had found a place where he felt at home. Felt needed.

"He's as miserable as you are."

Hope bloomed in her chest. "Did he say he missed me and Dani?"

"I heard it in his voice. I saw it in his eyes." José grew quiet.

"He won't come after you, because he believes you deserve better than him." José's piercing stare pinned Sara. "And you won't go after him, because you believe your love for Cruz dishonors Antonio and will hurt me."

He finally got the picture.

"I refuse to be the reason my daughter-in-law and granddaughter deny themselves the family they should have had all these years. I love my son and the two of you gave me a great gift when you had Dani. I'm sad that Antonio didn't appreciate you and Dani more, but there's no turning back the clock. You were a good wife to Antonio. A faithful wife. But now you must reach for your own happiness."

"José, I appreciate your understanding and compassion. But my job is here in Albuquerque. This city is full of bad memories for Cruz, and he won't return."

"You're a nurse. You can work anywhere."

"What are you saying?"

"Go to him."

"I can't live at the boys' ranch with Dani." She raised her hands in the air. "I don't even know where this ranch is."

Right then Sara's cell phone went off. She glanced at the number. "Alvarez Ranch for Boys." She looked at José suspiciously. "Hello.…Yes, this is Sara Mendez.…Yes, thank you for looking after my father-in-law, Maria."

José shoved his chair back and left the room. Ten minutes later Sara hung up and found José sitting on the porch steps. "You set this all up, didn't you?" Maria Fitzgerald had asked Sara if she'd be interested in running the health clinic at the ranch.

"No. Riley Fitzgerald mentioned that the ranch could use a nurse on the premises to help with injuries and illness. There are almost thirty boys living there and a few girls, too. Maria is working as both teacher and nurse."

"I can't take Dani to a place with troubled teens."

"There's a school on the property and plenty of room to build a small home for the three of you. I think Dani would love being around the horses and the boys would dote on her."

"You sure are changing your tune. I'm guessing some of the boys at the ranch have anger issues. It might not be safe there."

"Cruz wouldn't let anything happen to Dani. Besides, from what I saw, the boys looked up to Cruz and respected him."

Still…there was always the chance that one of the teens would fall back into their old ways and Dani might get caught in the middle of something that could hurt her.

"Sara."

"What?"

"Think with your heart, not your mind. Look where you live. There's danger all around you. Yes, this is a family neighborhood, but you're in the middle of the city. Anything can happen."

Her mind flashed back to the man in the window with a pistol by the Chinese restaurant she and Cruz had gone to. That had happened right in her backyard. What if Dani had been with them and the man had fired a gun? Her daughter could have gotten hurt.

"As much as I appreciate Maria's offer, I can't accept it," she said.

"Why not?"

"You just moved in with us. I'm not packing up and leaving you again. We're a family."

His eyes twinkled. "It won't be that easy to get rid of me. If you accept the job at the ranch, I'm going with you and I'll work in the camp kitchen. They're tired of hot dogs and beans. They want real Mexican food."

Sara squeezed her father-in-law's hand. He'd love making meals for the kids at the ranch. And if they could stay together…why not? Everything seemed to be falling into place. But there was just one problem. "What if we show up and you got it all wrong? What if Cruz doesn't want to be with me and Dani?" Sara didn't want to force him to leave the one place where he'd found refuge.

"You won't know unless you talk to Cruz. Tell him how you feel."

If she and Cruz were going to have a chance at a lasting relationship, she had to be the one to go after him. "What if it doesn't work out?"

"Then you, me and Dani are still a family."

For the first time in months Sara's heart lightened.

"Okay. I'm in," she said.

"In what, Mama?" Dani stood on the other side of the screen door rubbing her sleepy eyes.

"How would you like to live on a ranch with a lot of horses and bunch of boys?" Sara asked.

"I like horses, but I don't like boys."

José chuckled.

"If we're going to do this, I'd better give my two weeks' notice at work."

"I'll pack when you're at the clinic," José said.

"Why are we packing?" Dani asked.

"Mommy's taking a new job as a nurse on a ranch."

"What ranch?" Dani asked.

"The ranch Cruz works at."

"We get to see Mr. Cruz again?"

"Yes, we do, young lady."

"Yay!"

Win or lose, they were all in this together.

"LEAN LEFT, CARLOS!" Cruz shouted. The teen was being tossed around like a rag doll inside the corral. Fitzgerald had bought a new bucking horse for the ranch and the boys were waiting in line for a turn to ride.

All it took was three bucks and Carlos soared through the air. He got a mouthful of dirt when he landed. "I almost had him," the kid grumbled as he crawled to his feet.

"Almost is a long way from making it to eight," Cruz said.

The teen smiled as he limped over to Cruz. "He cheated."

Cruz chuckled. "All broncs cheat." He felt a special kinship with Carlos. The kid reminded him of his friend Alonso Marquez. Quiet, a little shy, but always willing to lend a hand. And he never had a bad word to say about anybody.

"Check out that girl." Carlos pointed over Cruz's shoulder. "Isn't she too young to be here?"

Cruz's breath caught in his chest. Even from fifty yards away he recognized Dani, her pigtails flying around her head as she took in all the action. His eyes shifted to Sara, who stood next to her SUV talking with Maria. José was engaged in a conversation with Fitzgerald.

"Do you know the little girl?" Carlos asked.

Cruz nodded. What were they doing here and why was there a trailer attached to the back of Sara's car?

He made a move to walk over to the group, but dang if his boot heels hadn't grown roots in the soil. His heart pumped hard in his chest and drawing air into his lungs took more effort than it should have.

"Is the lady your girlfriend?"

Girlfriend? He wanted to laugh. *Girlfriend* didn't come close to describing what he felt—still felt—for Sara.

"She's looking at you. Aren't you gonna talk to her?" Carlos nudged Cruz's arm.

"Yeah." Cruz forced his feet to move. Dani shouted his name, then raced toward him. Her bright smile eased some of the tension in him and he couldn't help himself from scooping her into his arms and twirling her in the air. There was no sweeter sound than her innocent laughter. Dani was everything good and right in the world. He set her on the ground, keeping a hand against her back as she teetered with dizziness. Then she wrapped her arms around his thigh and squeezed hard.

"Mama said we're gonna come live with you."

What? His gaze flew to Sara's. Her smile was guarded as she approached him.

"Dani, why don't you help José take our things to the guest cabin?"

"Then can I see the horses?"

"If Mr. Fitzgerald says it's okay." Sara tugged her daughter's braid. "Don't wander off alone anywhere."

"I won't." Dani raced back to her grandfather's side.

Cruz couldn't look away from Sara's face. He'd only left her a few weeks ago, but it seemed a lot longer than that as he stared into her blue eyes. Man, he'd forgotten how beautiful she was. His fingers twitched with the need to touch her. To caress her soft skin. Pull her close for a hug so he could bury his nose in her sweet-smelling hair.

"I imagine you're wondering what's going on," she said.

He nodded, not trusting his voice to break with emotion if he spoke.

"Maria and her husband asked me to run the health clinic at the ranch."

"What health clinic?" He forced the words past the lump in his throat.

"The one they're going to be building."

This was the first he'd heard about a new health clinic.

"And José will be working in the kitchen cooking for the boys. Maria says it's about time they hired someone who can make decent Mexican food."

Cruz struggled to wrap his head around what all this meant.

"Maria is going to help me homeschool Dani until she gets a little older. Then Dani can attend the ranch school with the other kids."

He was still speechless.

"I know you weren't expecting this. I don't even know if you want us here. But…"

Tears welled in her eyes and Cruz felt a crack spread through his chest. He yearned to hold her close, but he didn't know if that was what she wanted from him.

"I love you, Cruz. I didn't mean for it to happen." She shrugged. "I had enough on my plate trying to handle José and do what was best for him, my job and Dani. Then you came along and I tried not to let my guard down, but you slipped past my defenses. It wasn't until you left that I realized I'd fallen in love with you. And when you came back and found us stranded along the road, I knew that was my second chance and I had to give you a reason to stay with me…us." She wiped her eyes. "The night we went to dinner at the Chinese restaurant I was going to ask you to stay, but then there was that crazy guy wielding a gun, and then you told me you'd hung out with the Los Locos and I knew it was over for us. I couldn't be with you, because I believed it would upset José if he ever found out."

She didn't have to explain. Cruz had figured it all out on his own.

"Then José took off without telling me, and when he returned he said I'd be a fool not to go after you."

Cruz blinked hard, afraid he'd embarrass himself.

"So I'm here, Cruz. Telling you that I love you. Asking you to take a chance on loving me and Dani back."

"I don't have to take a chance, Sara. I already love you, but—"

She pressed her finger to his lips. "There are no buts, Cruz. Neither you or I can change the past. I can't bring my husband back to life. You can't decide not to wrestle the gun away from your friend or defend yourself in prison." She moved her finger to his cheek and stroked his skin. "All we can do is go on with our lives, but we can do it together, letting our love for each other heal us."

"Dani…" He swallowed hard. "It's not right that I should be a part of her life when…"

"Tony would approve." She spread her arms wide. "You're doing what he did, Cruz. Helping kids. You're trying to keep them on the right path. Tony would be thrilled to know I'm with someone who carries his dream of helping those in need. These boys won't get a second chance once they leave here. But with your help, my care and José's great cooking, we can do our best to make sure they don't waste the chance they've been given."

"Dani will miss her friends."

"She's already planning her birthday party out here with horse rides and a barbecue."

This couldn't be happening. What had he done to deserve the love of a woman like Sara and the trust of José and sweet Dani?

"Maria said once we get married they'll help us build our home on the property. She said there's a small grove near the school that blooms like crazy in the spring and it would be a pretty place for a house."

He caught Maria and Fitzgerald watching him and Sara…waiting for a signal that he was okay with the plans.

"If you don't want this, Cruz, tell me now, before I unpack the trailer."

"It's not that I don't want this." *Or don't want you.* "I want it more than you'll ever know, but I'm afraid."

"Of what?"

"Of disappointing you. Of not being what you thought I'd be. Of letting you, José and Dani down."

"You won't let us down."

"How do you know that?"

"Because you have all these people here who believe in you. Who've stood behind you through good and bad. They can't be wrong about you, Cruz. And if that's not good enough, then Dani telling me she wished you could be her father is enough proof that you'll never let us down."

"I don't deserve you or Dani," he whispered, opening his arms.

Sara snuggled close, the tears she'd held at bay escaping. "You deserve us and I'm going to show you every day just how much."

He leaned back and gazed into her eyes. "I love you, Sara. And I love Dani, too. I'll try hard to be a good father but I need you to tell me if I do something wrong." Hell, he didn't know the first thing about being a father.

"I don't need to tell you." She smiled. "Dani will let you know."

"You're sure José is okay with this?"

"You came into his life for a reason, too. I truly believe you're helping him move on, and he's finally gotten closure after Tony's death. He's got a new purpose now, cooking for the boys. He, too, feels like he's honoring Tony's memory. Tony would approve of the four of us becoming a family."

"Are you sure this is what you want?" It would be the hardest thing he'd ever done—including prison— to take a leap of faith and trust Sara when she said she wanted to be with him. But nothing in his life had followed a normal path or been easy, so why should this be any different?

"You are everything I need to be happy, and you came into my life for a reason. Maybe Tony had something to do with us meeting."

Cruz took comfort in her words and for the first time since they'd met, he allowed the door to his heart to open all the way and Sara slipped inside.

"So what do you say, Cruz Rivera?" Sara winked. "How about another go-round with me?"

He chuckled and pulled her close. "This is one ride I never want to end."

"Did he say yes?" Fitzgerald shouted.

Cruz gave a thumbs-up, then kissed Sara.

The future had looked pretty bleak when he'd gotten out of prison, but less than six months later he had more than most men found in their lifetime—true love and a family to call his own.

* * * * *

*Be sure to look for the next book
in Marin Thomas's*
COWBOYS OF THE RIO GRANDE *series
in December 2015!*

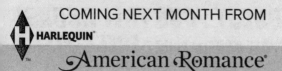

REQUEST YOUR FREE BOOKS!
2 FREE NOVELS PLUS 2 FREE GIFTS!

◊ HARLEQUIN®

American Romance®

LOVE, HOME & HAPPINESS

YES! Please send me 2 FREE Harlequin® American Romance® novels and my 2 FREE gifts (gifts are worth about $10). After receiving them, if I don't wish to receive any more books, I can return the shipping statement marked "cancel." If I don't cancel, I will receive 4 brand-new novels every month and be billed just $4.74 per book in the U.S. or $5.49 per book in Canada. That's a savings of at least 12% off the cover price! It's quite a bargain! Shipping and handling is just 50¢ per book in the U.S. and 75¢ per book in Canada.* I understand that accepting the 2 free books and gifts places me under no obligation to buy anything. I can always return a shipment and cancel at any time. Even if I never buy another book, the two free books and gifts are mine to keep forever.

154/354 HDN GHZZ

Name _____ (PLEASE PRINT)

Address _____ Apt. #

City _____ State/Prov. _____ Zip/Postal Code

Signature (if under 18, a parent or guardian must sign)

Mail to the **Reader Service:**
IN U.S.A.: P.O. Box 1867, Buffalo, NY 14240-1867
IN CANADA: P.O. Box 609, Fort Erie, Ontario L2A 5X3

Want to try two free books from another line?
Call 1-800-873-8635 or visit www.ReaderService.com.

* Terms and prices subject to change without notice. Prices do not include applicable taxes. Sales tax applicable in N.Y. Canadian residents will be charged applicable taxes. Offer not valid in Quebec. This offer is limited to one order per household. Not valid for current subscribers to Harlequin American Romance books. All orders subject to credit approval. Credit or debit balances in a customer's account(s) may be offset by any other outstanding balance owed by or to the customer. Please allow 4 to 6 weeks for delivery. Offer available while quantities last.

Your Privacy—The Reader Service is committed to protecting your privacy. Our Privacy Policy is available online at www.ReaderService.com or upon request from the Reader Service.

We make a portion of our mailing list available to reputable third parties that offer products we believe may interest you. If you prefer that we not exchange your name with third parties, or if you wish to clarify or modify your communication preferences, please visit us at www.ReaderService.com/consumerchoice or write to us at Reader Service Preference Service, P.O. Box 9062, Buffalo, NY 14240-9062. Include your complete name and address.

HARI5

*Daisy Donovan has finally decided to tell
John Lopez Mathison she loves him—but first she
must convince the people of Bridesmaids Creek
she's given up her wild ways!*

*Read on for a sneak preview of
THE COWBOY SEAL'S TRIPLETS,
the fourth book in **Tina Leonard**'s heartwarming
and hilarious series **BRIDESMAIDS CREEK**.*

Jane's gaze was steady on her. "John left town last night."

Daisy blinked. "Left town?"

The older woman hesitated, then sat across from her. Cosette Lafleur—Madame Matchmaker herself—slid in next to Jane, her pink-frosted hair accentuating her all-knowing eyes.

Daisy's heart sank. "He *couldn't* have left." He hadn't said goodbye, hadn't even mentioned he was planning to make like a stiff breeze and blow away.

The women stared at her with interest.

"Did you want him to stay, Daisy?" Jane asked.

"Well—" Daisy began, not knowing how to say that she'd thought she at least rated a "goodbye," considering she'd gotten quite in the habit of enjoying a nocturnal meeting in his arms. "It would have been nice."

"Have you finally realized where your heart belongs, Daisy?" Cosette asked, and Daisy started.

"My heart?" How was it that these women always seemed to read everyone's mind? A girl had to be very careful to keep her secrets tight to her chest. "Squint and I are friends."

Cosette winked at her, and a spark of hope lit inside her that maybe Cosette wasn't horribly angry or holding a grudge with her about the whole taking-over-her-shop thing.

"We know all about those kinds of friends," Cosette said, nodding wisely.

"Still," Jane said, "it does seem rather heartless of John to leave without telling you. Had you quarreled?"

Here it came, the well-meaning BC interference of which many suffered, all secretly cherished and she'd never had the benefit of experiencing. She had to say it was rather like being under a probing yet somehow friendly microscope. "We didn't quarrel."

"But you're in love with him," Cosette said.

"That may be putting it a bit—" Her words trailed off.

"Mildly?" Jane asked.

"Lightly?" Cosette said. "You are in fact head over heels in love with him?"

Daisy felt herself blush under all the scrutiny. Sheriff Dennis McAdams slid into the booth next to her, and the ladies wasted no time filling in the sheriff, who turned his curious gaze to her.

"He left last night," the sheriff said, and Daisy wondered if John Lopez Mathison had stopped by to see every single denizen of this town to say goodbye—except for her.

*Don't miss THE COWBOY SEAL'S TRIPLETS
by Tina Leonard, available July 2015
wherever Harlequin® American Romance®
books and ebooks are sold.*

www.Harlequin.com

Love the Harlequin book you just read?

Your opinion matters.

Review this book on your favorite book site, review site, blog or your own social media properties and share your opinion with other readers!

Be sure to connect with us at:
Harlequin.com/Newsletters
Facebook.com/HarlequinBooks
Twitter.com/HarlequinBooks

JUST CAN'T GET ENOUGH?

Join our social communities
and talk to us online.

You will have access to the latest
news on upcoming titles and special
promotions, but most importantly,
you can talk to other fans about your
favorite Harlequin reads.

Harlequin.com/Community

Facebook.com/HarlequinBooks

Twitter.com/HarlequinBooks

Pinterest.com/HarlequinBooks

HARLEQUIN®
A *Romance* FOR EVERY MOOD™

**Stay up-to-date on all your
romance-reading news with the
Harlequin Shopping Guide,
featuring bestselling authors, exciting new
miniseries, books to watch and more!**

The newest issue will be delivered right to you
with our compliments! There are 4 each year.

Signing up is easy.

EMAIL

ShoppingGuide@Harlequin.ca

WRITE TO US

HARLEQUIN BOOKS
Attention: Customer Service Department
P.O. Box 9057, Buffalo, NY 14269-9057

OR PHONE

1-800-873-8635 in the United States
1-888-343-9777 in Canada

Please allow 4-6 weeks for delivery of the first issue by mail.

THE WORLD IS BETTER WITH

Romance

Harlequin has everything from contemporary, passionate and heartwarming to suspenseful and inspirational stories.

Whatever your mood, we have a romance just for you!

Connect with us to find your next great read, special offers and more.

⊕ HARLEQUIN®

A *Romance* FOR EVERY MOOD™

www.Harlequin.com